KU-431-624

AT THE HIGHLANDER'S MERCY

Terri Brisbin

KENT
ARTS & LIBRARIES

All the characters in this book have no existence outside the imagination of the author, and have no relation whatsoever to anyone bearing the same name or names. They are not even distantly inspired by any individual known or unknown to the author, and all the incidents are pure invention.

All Rights Reserved including the right of reproduction in whole or in part in any form. This edition is published by arrangement with Harlequin Enterprises II BV/S.à.r.l. The text of this publication or any part thereof may not be reproduced or transmitted in any form or by any means, electronic or mechanical, including photocopying, recording, storage in an information retrieval system, or otherwise, without the written permission of the publisher.

® and TM are trademarks owned and used by the trademark owner and/or its licensee. Trademarks marked with ® are registered with the United Kingdom Patent Office and/or the Office for Harmonisation in the Internal Market and in other countries.

First published in Great Britain 2013
by Mills & Boon, an imprint of Harlequin (UK) Limited.
Large Print edition 2013
Harlequin (UK) Limited, Eton House, 18-24 Paradise Road,
Richmond, Surrey TW9 1SR

© Theresa S. Brisbin 2013

ISBN: 978 0 263 23278 3

Harlequin (UK) policy is to use papers that are natural, renewable and recyclable products and made from wood grown in sustainable forests. The logging and manufacturing process conform to the legal environmental regulations of the country of origin.

Printed and bound in Great Britain
by CPI Antony Rowe, Chippenham, Wiltshire

'Who are you? Why have you done this?' she said as she looked from one man to another and to the next. 'Does my father know about this?'

Rob waited for her to bring her gaze back to him and then he smiled at her.

A silent moment passed, and then another, before the light of recognition flared in her forest-green eyes. Then she shook her head, though whether in disbelief or confusion he knew not. Lilidh opened her mouth several times but no words escaped. The distraction was all he needed to gain control of her, so he crossed the empty space between them in a few paces, grabbed her wrist and squeezed until she dropped the dagger. Kicking it aside, he still held on to her. As she probably had when Symon took her, she did not allow his hold to remain there. She began backing away, pulling and tugging, trying to free herself.

Lilidh just did not realise she had no chance of escape. As Dougal and some others returned to the hall Rob gave one sharp tug and pulled her close, wrapping his arms around her from behind. He noticed the smell of blood and saw the thick patch of it on her head—she had been struck and knocked unconscious. Tightening his hold, he leaned down and whispered in her ear, so that only she could hear his words.

''Tis good to see you, too, Lilidh. It's been a long time.'

AUTHOR NOTE

More than five years ago, while I was writing POSSESSED BY THE HIGHLANDER, the heroine's daughter surprised me by grabbing her mother's hand and declaring her intention to marry the young man who had been entertaining her during their journey to their new home. In a flash I saw Ciara Robertson as a grown woman, marrying Tavis MacLerie, the man she claimed in that moment! Fast forward to 2013 and I'm thrilled to have had the chance to tell their story in my last book, THE HIGHLANDER'S STOLEN TOUCH, and now to watch as all the children born in the first three tales find their own love stories.

Connor and Jocelyn, Rurik and Margriet and Duncan and Marian—the heroes and heroines from my first trilogy—must find suitable matches for them...and that leads to a challenge among the couples about the mothers or fathers finding the best spouses for their children!

So, I hope you'll enjoy returning to the powerful MacLerie laird, his lady, kith and kin as they face the challenges and rewards of life in Lairig Dubh, Scotland!

Terri Brisbin is wife to one, mother of three, and dental hygienist to hundreds when not living the life of a glamorous romance author. She was born, raised and is still living in the southern New Jersey suburbs. Terri's love of history led her to write time-travel romances and historical romances set in Scotland and England.

Readers are invited to visit her website for more information at www.terribrisbin.com, or contact her at PO Box 41, Berlin, NJ 08009-0041, USA.

Previous novels by the same author:

THE DUMONT BRIDE
LOVE AT FIRST STEP
  (short story in *The Christmas Visit*)
THE NORMAN'S BRIDE
THE COUNTESS BRIDE
THE EARL'S SECRET
TAMING THE HIGHLANDER
SURRENDER TO THE HIGHLANDER
POSSESSED BY THE HIGHLANDER
BLAME IT ON THE MISTLETOE
  (short story in *One Candlelit Christmas*)
THE MAID OF LORNE
THE CONQUEROR'S LADY*
THE MERCENARY'S BRIDE*
HIS ENEMY'S DAUGHTER*
THE HIGHLANDER'S STOLEN TOUCH†

and in Mills & Boon® Historical *Undone!* eBooks:

A NIGHT FOR HER PLEASURE*

And in M&B:

PRINCE CHARMING IN DISGUISE
  (part of *Royal Weddings Through the Ages*)

*The Knights of Brittany
†The MacLerie Clan

**Did you know that some of these novels
are also available as eBooks?
Visit www.millsandboon.co.uk**

Chapter One

Lilidh MacLerie, eldest daughter of the MacLerie laird and Earl of Douran, looked out her window and tried to sort through her options. This silent time between the gloaming and the night was her favourite when she needed to make decisions or choices. Remembering now that she'd made the decision that had brought her to this time and place made her pause. Mayhap she should wait until morning instead?

Turning from the window and gazing across the large, well-furnished chamber, she knew she had little time or choice…again. The parchment remained as she'd left it and she lifted it, tilting it so that the light of several candles made it able to be read. For the fiftieth time, she said the words and could not yet decide what else to write, when so much more was needed.

To the Earl and Countess of Douran, it began, using their formal titles first. *Father and Mother,* next.

And then the words disappeared.

How could she explain the private misery behind the very public death of her husband of only two months? The MacGregor's death had been kept quiet for now until his heir, his younger brother, was approved by the clan elders as chief. Her purpose in this marriage—to bind their clans and to produce an heir for the MacGregor—was a failure. Though, even as an innocent young woman coming to this marriage, she understood that things were not as they should have been between her and Iain MacGregor.

The parchment in her hand moved in the current of the warm air created by the heat of the candles and reminded her that this task also went unfinished. Sitting at the table, she lifted the quill, dabbed the ink so it would not splatter and forced the words on to the page that would both embarrass and humiliate her in her parents' and clan's eyes.

I find myself in need of your counsel concerning the situation of my position here in Iain

MacGregor's household and family. As his widow, though with no hope of producing an heir, I know...

What did she know? She had married him under a contract negotiated by her uncle and signed by her father. Her dower portion was protected for her use and she had been given the choice of remaining here as part of her husband's clan or to return to her own. Her uncle had made certain to protect her in the contract, but giving her such a choice made things more difficult than if she'd been simply told what to do.

If she remained, there would be another marriage arranged for her, to a suitable eligible man, to keep the bonds between the clans strong. If she returned home, there would be another marriage, but also she would face the disappointment of her family in her failure. And with no way to explain and with no one to speak candidly about it, what could she say? Lilidh dipped the quill again to freshen the ink and placed the tip of it on the parchment.

She was being a silly ninny. Her parents loved her and would accept her back, explanation or not. Her mother was the only one to whom she could speak on personal matters. As she had before her marriage, even if that conversation did not explain what had happened or, as it was, not happened between a husband and wife. Looking off at the flame of the candle, she took and released a deep breath, and did the only sensible thing she could: she asked leave to come home.

I find little reason to remain here and would ask your permission to return to Lairig Dubh as soon as an escort can be arranged. I would seek your counsel on other important personal matters, but I hesitate to put them in this letter.

Father, please send word if this is your pleasure.

Mother, please keep me in your prayers and ask the Almighty to watch over me during this trying time.

It was short, but to the point, and there truly was little else to say in her missive. Sanding it, Lilidh allowed the ink to dry and then folded the letter, sealing it with the ring her father had given her on the anniversary of her birth a year before. She would send it off on the morrow with one of the MacLerie servants who had accompanied her here. Hopefully, within a fortnight, she would have an answer from her parents and know what her future held for her.

But how could she explain that though she was a bride and a widow, she'd never been a wife?

Jocelyn MacCallum, wife to Connor MacLerie, held the parchment before her and read it once more. The sadness in her daughter's words was clear to her. Lilidh, her eldest daughter, was never anything but confident and self-assured. But the words, nay, the tone of this latest letter, told her that Lilidh was lost.

'You will give her permission?' she asked her husband as he climbed from their bed and walked to where she sat. As she glanced up, her mother's heart grew heavy in her chest. Lilidh was far away and all Jocelyn wanted to do was to take her in her arms and soothe away the pain that was so evident in her words.

'I am discussing it with Duncan and the other elders,' Connor replied quietly as he lifted the parchment and placed it back on the table. 'The MacGregors have kept Iain's death quiet until his heir is in place. With tensions so high and war with their rival clan the MacKenzies in the air, they do not wish to open themselves to attack. But, for this night, there is nothing to be done, Jocelyn. Come back to bed.' He took her hand in his and entwined their fingers, tugging her to stand.

She allowed her husband to wrap her in his arms, much as she wanted to do to Lilidh, but Jocelyn realised quickly that his aim had little to do with comforting a lost child. She caught her breath as he lifted her in his strong arms and carried her back to their bed. She understood that her husband's need for her as well as his attempts to distract her from her sadness and taking too much interest in clan decisions brought on his intimate attentions. She'd allow it, later, for those same reasons.

For now, she asked her last question once more, not content to let the men make this critical decision without her counsel.

'Will you bring her home?' She watched as many emotions crossed her husband's face, but the final one that settled was acceptance. As she knew it would.

'Aye. I was simply waiting on her word.'

She leaned into him and kissed his mouth. 'Did

you send her word yet?' He pulled her close, surrounding her with his strength and his love. Kissing her forehead, he rested his chin on her head.

'The message to the MacGregor will go out on the morrow. She should be home in a sennight.'

'And the implications?' she asked. This marriage arrangement had been between clans and chiefs and not simply between a man and woman. And it had been part of their, the fathers' and the mothers', wager to find the best match for their children. Since this involved her daughter, Jocelyn had been left out of most discussions, except for the private ones she'd had with Connor. Ones that always seemed to end up with them in bed!

'You know the implications. No questions have been raised to me about her involvement in Iain's death, so the MacGregors must be at peace with how it happened. Her dowry will be returned to us and any future marriages will be at my discretion.'

Those were the words she wanted to hear. Lilidh would return home to her family and her future happiness would again be in her father's hands, along with the counsel of his closest relatives and advisers…and her.

But since Jocelyn had thought this marriage a good one, she could little complain about Connor's choice. Whatever had happened—between Iain and Lilidh and to cause his death—had ended any chance that it could prove out.

Comforting done, Connor lifted his head and touched their mouths together. In only moments, the passion between them flared and Jocelyn savoured it. This is what she'd hoped Lilidh would find in her marriage. Even though older and married before, Iain had seemed a kind soul and appeared to worship Lilidh. Their betrothal and marriage showed promise and Jocelyn had no doubt that she would soon have grandchildren from the match.

Now, Iain was dead and Lilidh returning home.

She would get to the real reasons and to the true situation once she had Lilidh back and they could speak plainly. Her letter asked for such counsel, almost begged for it, and she would help her daughter in any way she could.

But, for now, her husband demanded her attentions and when the Beast of the Highlands called to his mate, she always answered.

Always.

* * *

Robert Matheson clenched his teeth until he thought they would crumble under the pressure. Anything, anything to keep from letting his anger and frustration spill out the way he wanted to. Clenching his fists did not help either and finally he could not allow this madness to continue.

'Halt!' he called out to those bickering before him. 'Attacking the MacLeries will lead only to our destruction.' Looking from one to the next, he met their gazes and realised the futility of trying to stop them. If he could not stop them, he must delay them. 'If we are to do so, we must have a plan and ready ourselves. It cannot be done as quickly as you would like.' Or as easily as they thought.

The Matheson clan elders had approved him as chief when his father passed, but it had been a hard-won battle. His cousin, Symon, the son of his father's older sister, had been in contention and was suited for the warmongers among the councillors. Rob, on the other hand, had a clear understanding of the strength and power and fighting might of the MacLerie clan for he had spent years among them.

As Connor MacLerie's foster son.

Rob had lived for five years with them, learning his own fighting skills from the best of their warriors, learning battle strategies from their tacticians and the ways to prevent battles from their negotiator. Now, he had no intention of leaping into a fight with a clan he could not defeat. Or worse, with a clan who would destroy them and leave not a piece of wood or stone standing on their lands. Though listening to some on the council drone on and on about all the reasons they should and listening to those who knew nothing and understood less made him think about letting them all charge into the fray unprepared.

Still, his innate loyalty to his family, kith and kin stopped him from goading them into such an act. Glancing at his other cousin, Dougal, the one who did not wish to be laird, he waited for the only person with some sense to speak up and support his plan. Dougal did and though those wanting war did not quiet completely, it did make them listen.

'Robbie is right,' Dougal called out, gaining their attention. 'To rush in against such a clan will result in all our deaths.' Some grumbled at his declaration, but the others quieted and waited on his words. 'Let the *laird* study this and make the necessary plans. Hear him out when he does for no one knows the MacLeries as he does. If there is a weakness to be found, he is the one to find it.' His voice rang out in the silence, but Rob did not know whether to cheer or to strangle him.

The best way to defeat the MacLerie? The Beast of the Highlands?

There was none.

Rob's actions so far must even be considered a betrayal of their bond by Connor. Attacking would simply be a death warrant for him and the rest of the Mathesons. The only weakness the man had was for his children and, other than that, he was ruthless in weeding out enemies and dealing with betrayal. Breaking his ties with Connor at the behest of the council and currying favour with the MacKenzies had been the hardest thing he'd ever done. He did not doubt there would be hell to pay over it.

Dougal finished and stepped back, allowing Rob to move to the centre of the dais while the men were yet calm.

'I have been gathering information already,'

he said. 'Even now, I've sent messengers out to determine their weaknesses and vulnerabilities. In a few days or a sennight at the most, we will meet and prepare our plans.'

He dismissed them with his most imperious wave, hoping they would obey—and they did. All save Dougal left him in peace. He returned to the table and filled his goblet with ale. When Rob turned back, Dougal remained. He poured another goblet and handed it to his cousin, the one who did not wish to be laird.

'You sounded convincing, Rob,' Dougal said. He drank a couple of mouthfuls and then wiped his mouth with his arm. 'Do you have a plan?'

'Other than praying to the Almighty for a flood?'

'You had that look in your eyes,' Dougal said laughing. 'You never could bluff.' Dougal met his gaze and all mirth disappeared. 'What will you do?'

'Stall for more time,' Rob said. 'I cannot figure out why they want to go up against the MacLeries. Come now—I cannot be the only one who knows their strength?'

Rob drank deeply, watching the servants in the

hall preparing for the evening meal. It was not as spacious or well appointed a hall as the one at Lairig Dubh, but it was his. He'd sworn an oath to protect his family and if it had to be from themselves, so be it. Something more was going on here, something he could feel, but could not see, and getting the real reason why some in the clan wanted to ally them with the MacKenzies and break all past ties with the MacLeries was critical.

'How can I help?' Dougal asked, putting the now-empty goblet down on the table.

They both watched as a comely maid approached and took the goblet and the pitcher to refill it. Unmarried and one of the most beautiful of his cousins, removed by several generations, Ellyn smiled at them and sauntered away, her shapely hips moving in a rhythm meant to entice and draw attention. A moment or two passed before they regained their senses and their subject.

'As I said, how can I help?' Dougal repeated.

Rob looked at his closest friend and decided he must trust someone in this matter before everything went out of control. Stepping closer, he lowered his voice.

'Someone is behind this effort to make the MacLeries our enemies. Though not friends or enemies of the MacKenzies, they avoid each other's areas of concern and properties. So this intentional goading is not something either one wants and not something we can afford to get in the middle of now.' He paused and checked to see who was near them. Seeing no one, he said, 'I suspect that my cousin Symon is the one, but without proof, I cannot accuse.'

Dougal studied him and then nodded. 'I will see what I can do.'

Rob smacked his shoulder. 'I will be in your debt.'

Dougal strode off, leaving Rob behind to deal with the other matters that faced a clan chief and laird every day. Complaints from villagers. Requests from the clan. Demands from the elders that he marry his betrothed—Symon's sister— as his bride sooner to unite the two fighting factions. And on and on each day.

When he had been fostered by Connor, he'd never dreamt of being in this position—chief of his family and in charge of their holdings. The laird, his natural father, was hardy and young enough to produce a male heir in addition to the lasses he'd had with several wives. With his new wife heavily pregnant, the expectation was that a son would be born. A direct, legitimate heir.

As son of the laird's older sister, Symon should have had no expectations other than being counsellor to the next laird, or to serve him in some capacity. As the laird's bastard, Rob's expectations were lower still. Now, his father and his wife were dead in an accident and Rob, illegitimate or not, had been chosen to lead the clan.

And his cousin Symon, legitimate or not, was not.

As Rob watched Dougal make his way out of the hall, he knew Dougal would find out the truth. In the meantime, Rob needed to gather those loyal to him and be ready to head off this foolish attempt—both to usurp his position, a position he'd discovered he truly did want, and to throw the existing treaties with the MacLeries and the MacKenzies into disarray.

He prayed only that there was time before the disaster he could feel in his bones arrived on his doorstep.

Chapter Two

Lilidh turned to the right, trying to decide if she truly was seeing someone moving along their path in the shadows or if it was a trick of the light and the leaves. She peered into the darkness of the forest and watched more carefully for a few moments. Not certain, she rode on, never mentioning it to either of her companions or their guards. Then, just as they followed the turn in the road that would take them south to Lairig Dubh, the attack came.

One moment they were riding quietly along and in the next, the men descended from the hills around them and, though Lilidh was a good rider, she found herself unhorsed and standing encircled by five armed warriors. She gazed at them as she drew her dagger. She would fight them if only her leg would remain strong.

And she did, turning the handle of her blade in her palm for a better grip and swiping it around her to keep them from getting too close too quickly. Glancing around to see how the others fared, Lilidh realised only she remained standing while the rest lay scattered around the area either dead or unconscious. She took a deep breath and tried to run, but someone grabbed her from behind and dragged her up against their large, muscular body. Like being thrown against a rock wall, it forced the air from her body. A beefy hand entangled in her loosened hair and her head was dragged back. With her neck exposed so, she knew it was only a matter of moments before she died. Offering up a silent prayer asking for forgiveness of her sins, she waited for the death-blow to strike.

'Who is she?' a gruff voice demanded from beside her. The one holding her turned their bodies as one until she could see her maid across the clearing. Or at least her lifeless body as one of the other men touched her with his foot.

Isla made no sound and did not move. Lilidh drew in a ragged breath at the possibility that the older woman who had helped raise her was dead.

Her eyes burned with tears, but then her anger rose at such a thought. The woman was there to see to her comfort and now lay dead because... Because of what? Of whom? The daughter of the Beast of the Highlands felt his pride rise in her blood.

'Who are you to attack those travelling under the MacLerie banner?' she asked, struggling to pull free. 'What do you want?'

One of the men broke away from the others and strode towards her. The expression in his dark gaze made her take a step back, but the taller man behind her was like a wall that kept her in place. 'You are the MacLerie's girl.'

It wasn't a question so Lilidh did not answer. Her chin lifted. Her pride would not allow her to slink away or hide her heritage. Still, she would know who dared to attack them.

'And who are you? Why do you need to kill an innocent woman?' she said, refusing to cry out as the man holding her prisoner wrenched her head back with a rough tug.

The dark-eyed man nodded to the one holding her and the other one nearer to Isla. She opened her mouth to demand her freedom when the blow hit her from behind and her world went black.

Each of the next several days went from bad to something that resembled his idea of hell. Rob managed to calm one faction of his family only to have another rise up in complaint. He wondered many times through those last days how Connor MacLerie made it look so easy. Peering over the rim of his goblet as yet another storm brewed in his hall, Rob realised that the one thing that Connor had to help him was his terrible reputation, one not completely undeserved, as the murderous Beast of the Highlands. As he glanced from one squawking Matheson to another, he considered murdering them all and gaining himself a similar reputation.

Symon had been quieter than usual, but that only worried Rob more. At least when he was making noise or complaining, he knew what Symon was up to. His cousin had been absent from the keep and village without word. A worrying thing, that.

He was about to summon Dougal when the doors to the hall were thrown open and a large group of warriors, under Symon's control and with him in the lead, came crashing in, yelling and calling out to each other as though celebrating some great victory. Rob nodded to the man he'd appointed as his commander and by the time his cousin and the others reached the front of the hall, additional soldiers had entered and taken positions around the chamber. If Symon noticed, he did not say, but his swagger and manners spoke of trouble walking towards him.

'Rob,' Dougal said as he approached from the other side. He took his place behind his laird as Symon reached the dais. 'He is up to nothing good.' Rob only nodded, never taking his gaze off the seething group of men, and waited. The attack was not long in coming.

'You have dragged your heels long enough, *Laird*,' Symon began, using his title as a curse. 'The Mathesons will not serve a leader who will not lead them.'

Shouts both for and against him rippled through the men gathered there and they gained the attention of anyone who might have otherwise passed on through, carrying out their duties. Soon an even larger audience listened to Symon's threats to his position as chief. Symon waited and then waved them quiet.

'It matters not now, for I have done what you could not and would not do.'

After making that challenge to his leadership, Symon walked forwards and climbed the first step. Rob blocked him from moving forwards. Every man in the hall tensed and the air seethed with discontent and hostility. Dougal's hand moved to the hilt of his sword, but Rob shook his head, holding him from taking that step.

'I care not for your words, Symon,' Rob said, stepping down and forcing Symon to move back. He did. 'I am chief and will make decisions for this clan.'

Crossing his arms over his chest, he watched Symon's expression as all those loyal to him lined up behind Rob. All the elders save one, Murtagh, gathered with him, but Murtagh's move was not a surprise to Rob. The old man had supported Symon's claim throughout the time of uncertainty and did not yield now.

'You refuse to take action against the MacLeries, though we want it,' Symon said. Rob's gut seized, warning of something bad coming. The next words confirmed it. 'Lachlan, come,' he called.

Symon motioned with his hand and his men separated. One of the men strode forwards from the back of the hall while Symon's gaze never left his. Lachlan carried a bundle over his shoulder and Rob could not guess what it contained. Then he saw the bundle move, much as a body would if carried in that manner, and he drew a breath through his clenched teeth.

'Symon,' he whispered, 'what have you done?'

He turned from the self-satisfied smirk of his cousin and towards the man and the bundle. Taking no care, Lachlan dropped it on the rush-covered floor just in front of them and stepped back. This was not going to end well, for neither him nor the person they'd kidnapped.

'You have orchestrated this. Carry on, Symon, and let us see who lies within,' he said. Better to see what challenge he faced then drag this out, he thought.

Symon, not a small man, though not as large as Lachlan, walked to the bundle, untied the ropes encircling it and tugged an end free. With a grip on that and one good flick, the bundle unrolled and unrolled until a woman was freed and left lying at their feet.

A woman who had ropes around her wrists and ankles and a sack over her head. A woman who did not move now, in spite of Symon's prodding foot. A woman who had suffocated to death from their harsh treatment?

'What the hell did you do, Symon?' he shouted as he bent over the woman. Tugging the sack off her head and then removing the gag he found there, he summoned one of the women over to see to her as he stood and dragged Symon aside. 'Who is this and why did you kidnap her?'

'We did not kidnap her, Rob. She is a prisoner of war,' he said.

'We are not at war,' Rob said as one possibility began to tease his thoughts. Even Symon would not be so bold and brash as to… Nay! It could not be. Was it truly Lilidh MacLerie?

Rob had turned back to look at the woman who lay unconscious on his floor. The servant had pushed her hair from her face and was dabbing at her dirt-covered face with a wet cloth. He took in the costliness of her clothing and the jewelled rings on her hand, not missing the gold band that spoke of her married state.

Then he noticed the gently arching brows, the curve of her neck and the full lips that had enticed him even in his youth and yet haunted his dreams—and he knew it was her.

'You kidnapped the MacLerie's daughter? She is wed to Iain MacGregor.'

He swore under his breath now as the implications hit him. This was an act of war against two powerful clans. Worse, this was not simply taking their cattle or burning a few farms, which would be insult enough. This was a personal attack as well on both clans and their chiefs. Holy Christ, what had Symon got them into now?

'Dougal, check the guards. Brodie,' he called to the steward, 'get the outlying families into the village and gather the stores.'

He pushed Symon aside and walked over to take a closer look at Lilidh. As he could have predicted, she'd fought against them when they took her—the bruises on her face and her torn fingernails showed that much. The markings of a man's fingers on her neck made his own clench in response. What else had they done to her?

'How did you find her?' he asked, as he strode towards Symon. Nothing, nothing would give him greater pleasure now than pounding his face into the floor and breaking a few of his bones. Grabbing Symon by the neck, he forced him back several steps until his back met the wall behind him. 'Where are the others?'

Symon's gaze moved to something or someone over Rob's shoulder and Rob knew Lachlan approached. With a nod of his head, his men took care of that threat. 'Where are they?' he asked again, squeezing hard until Symon choked for breath.

'She was returning to Lairig Dubh. We took her on the road just after the river as she left the MacGregors' lands,' he forced out.

'And her guards? Her servants?' No daughter of the MacLerie and wife of the MacGregor would travel alone.

'A few of the guards are dead. We left the rest of them and took their horses.'

'Did they see you?' he asked, but he knew the answer. They made sure they could be identified as Mathesons. Symon wanted the MacLeries and

MacGregors to know who'd taken Lilidh. They wanted to force his hand into war.

He tossed Symon to the ground and turned back to the servant at Lilidh's side. 'Find a chamber for her.'

'She is my prisoner, Rob. I want her held in the aerie.'

'You think she is that dangerous?' he asked, pointing to the unconscious woman on the floor.

The aerie was in one of the oldest parts of the keep and sat open to the winds. Lightning had struck the roof and blown it away and no one had ever repaired it. Though mostly unused, it had been used as a cell for prisoners in the past... the far, far past. Rob turned back to argue with Symon and to assert his control over any prisoner of the clan when she moved.

Within a few moments, she'd seized a dagger from one of his men and held the servant woman hostage. The wild expression in her eyes spoke of her confusion, but warned him of her uncertain behaviour. Spreading his hands out to show he was unarmed, he began to walk towards her slowly and evenly.

'Here now, lass,' Rob said softly. 'Let Edith go and all will be well.'

His words might have worked until Symon began jeering at her and his men added their taunts. Overwhelmed and injured, she glanced left and right, estimating her escape routes, he was sure. She dragged Edith with her, using her as a shield as she moved. When Lilidh blinked several times and stumbled, Rob suspected a head injury. He tried to follow her moves, staying the same distance from her and speaking quietly to her, but his voice was drowned out by Symon's men.

'Silence!' he yelled, trying to regain control over a dangerous situation.

Well, he did manage to get the men under control but it gave Lilidh the moment she was watching and waiting for and she pushed Edith at him and ran for the door. He passed Edith off once she regained her balance and ran to catch up with her before she got to the door or before Symon reached her. Symon was faster and he got between her and the door, forcing her to stop. He wondered how she could move so quickly on her leg.

'Come now,' Symon urged her towards him. 'Do you want to try me again?' he goaded.

Rob swore he would kill Symon for this, but first he must stop Lilidh before she was seriously hurt. He doubted that Lilidh knew where she was or even who he was. No glimmer of recognition filled her eyes when their gazes met, but years had passed since she'd seen him last and he'd done the usual growing up that young men did. No matter the manner of their parting, he would never forget what she looked like. Turning his attentions back to her, he decided that he would need to gain her trust.

'Lilidh MacLerie,' he called out to her. 'Do you remember me?' he asked while waving Symon off. When his men positioned themselves to intervene, Symon finally backed off, though the expression in his eyes promised it was not the end of his challenge to Rob's leadership. 'Lilidh?'

Her hand, holding the dagger out before her, began to shake badly and she lost her balance once more. Just when he thought she would tumble to the floor, she righted herself and pushed her hair out of her eyes and tried to focus on him.

'Who are you? Why have you done this?' she

said as she looked from one man to another and to the next. 'Does my father know about this?' Rob waited for her to bring her gaze back to him and then he smiled at her.

A silent moment passed and then another and another before the light of recognition flared in her forest-green eyes. Then she shook her head, though whether in disbelief or confusion he knew not. Lilidh opened her mouth several times, but no words escaped. The distraction was all he needed to gain control of her without hurting her more so he crossed the empty space between them in a few paces, grabbed her wrist and squeezed until she dropped the dagger. Kicking it aside, he still held on to her. As she probably had when Symon took her, she did not allow his hold to remain there. She began backing away, pulling and tugging, trying to free herself.

Lilidh just did not realise she had no chance of escape. As Dougal and some others returned to the hall, he gave one sharp tug and pulled her close, wrapping his arms around her from behind. Rob noticed the smell of blood and saw the thick patch of it on her head—she had been struck and knocked unconscious. Tightening his hold on her, he leaned down and whispered in her ear so that only she could hear his words.

'Lilidh, you are safe with me. No one will hurt you.'

All the times he'd dreamt of holding her in his arms he had never seen it happening this way. But his body reacted, regardless of how and why, as he felt the womanly curves resting under his arms. Once she realised who he was, any chance of holding her like this would disappear for ever. She belonged to another man and could never be his. She was the daughter of a powerful chief and he was a bastard pretending to be laird.

It would never be, so why not make that clear from this moment on? Taking in a breath, he spoke the words that would separate them for ever...again.

'Lilidh, it's me, Rob Matheson.'

Her body stiffened for a moment and then she tried to turn to look at him. He relaxed his grip a tiny bit to allow her to do that. Her green gaze searched his face, seeing the changes that growing up and fighting had wrought there, and he watched as her expression changed. The fear remained, but shock entered it now and she trembled again. It only took a few seconds before the next emotion filled those beautiful green eyes and it was the one he was hoping for. It would help her survive whatever happened around them.

Anger. Her eyes filled and flashed with it and her hand lifted as he'd expected it to. Although she swung with all her might, he captured it easily and held it between them.

''Tis good to see you, too, Lilidh. It's been a long time,' he goaded her a-purpose.

'You bastard,' she swore at him. 'You are behind this?'

Before he could answer, Dougal called out to him.

'Some of the villagers come. The gates are secured,' Dougal said as he approached, not missing the lovely woman still in his arms. 'This is the MacLerie's daughter, then?' he asked, his appreciative gaze clear to everyone watching.

'Aye. His eldest girl.' Rob pitched his voice to sound uninterested.

'And you two are acquainted?' he asked, meeting Rob's glance.

'Do not be a fool, Dougal. Here…' he held out Lilidh's hand towards the man and pushed her closer '…put her some place for now.' Dougal's gaze narrowed and he looked from him to Lilidh and back again.

'Symon said the aerie. Is that where you want her?' Dougal watched him closely as he asked his pointed, probing questions.

Where did he want her? In his bed, naked, was the first place he thought of, but the one he could never admit. Shaking his head to clear the lust from his thoughts, he considered the aerie, with its position high in the old tower, one that could be approached by only one stairwell and would be easily defended. Putting her there would keep Symon satisfied and make him less of a problem. And, if her family came calling sooner than he expected, her position there would make them think twice before assaulting the keep.

Hell! What was he thinking?

The aerie was barbaric with its open walls, cracked wooden roof and nothing in the way of comfort. Putting her there would be another way to tweak the MacLeries and the MacGregors into acting against him faster than they already would. Rob stepped away from Dougal and Lilidh and dragged his hands through his hair.

The others stood watching and waiting on his word—Symon, Dougal, his men, the elders, all the others who called him chief and those who would remove him with but a wrong word.

'Take her to my chambers,' he ordered quietly, hating the way that Dougal's right eyebrow lifted in silent censure, but not willing to deny it.

The hall erupted with shouts from those backing Symon and those backing him. He would bring this under control and make Lilidh hate him even more than she probably did at this moment.

'She is my prisoner!' Symon demanded, shaking his fist at Rob. Rob quickly and without warning strode over to Symon and punched him in the jaw, knocking him to the floor as he'd wanted to do for days.

'I am chief here and she is my prisoner. You wanted to anger the MacLerie and draw him into a fight? 'Twas your thought that kidnapping her would do it? Well, you have brought her here and she is mine now. Taking her to my bed will be even more effective in drawing him here.'

'I will not be—' Lilidh began to say but he gave her no time to say more. Rob turned and was in front of her before she could finish any declaration she would make.

To show her, to show them, who was in charge, he grabbed her by the shoulders and lifted her to him, taking her mouth in a claiming kiss that told one and all that he would possess her body and soul before this was done. His demonstration was so successful that all of them began to cheer and urge him on.

Her mouth that was closed against his now softened and he deepened the kiss, tasting the sweetness he had craved for years. Tasting the passion that had lay dormant between them for so many reasons. Reasons that were important then, but now flew off like a flock of summer geese in the autumn's chill. His thoughts scattered as his body reacted to her mouth and the enticing way she touched her tongue to his.

Until she latched on to the tip of his and bit him! Chiding himself for losing his mind under the guise of putting on a show for those watching, he pushed her back into Dougal's arms and laughed as he wiped blood from his mouth. Blood she'd drawn.

'Symon, you wait for me in the solar. Dougal,

put her in my chambers. Use a rope or chains if you need to keep her there. I will see to her later,' he ordered.

Lilidh didn't say a word as Dougal led her away, but the expression now in her eyes resembled the one in Symon's eyes just minutes ago. One that promised death and mayhem—with him as the target.

He turned away to see to another task before dealing with those challenging his position and wondered if he or his clan would survive this encounter with Lilidh MacLerie.

Chapter Three

She tried to walk to his chambers, tried to keep her anger inflamed, but her strength—and her leg—gave out by the time they reached the second flight of steps leading up into the tower. Lilidh would have fallen down had it not been for Rob's man who caught her and carried her the rest of the way. The dizziness that came in waves and inundated her senses did not help. Any strength she mustered to continue to fight him leached away as she was overwhelmed by pain and exhaustion.

And somewhere in that mix of emotions, confusion, anger and a bit of relief swirled. No matter the news she'd received about the Mathesons' breaking their agreements with the MacLeries, and no matter the personal rift between her and Rob, she knew he would never cause her harm.

No matter that kiss and his threat to take her to his bed... Her body shivered, chills and flames travelling through her at the memory of his mouth possessing hers. The Matheson called Dougal shifted her in his arms and turned down another corridor.

'We are nearly there,' he said quietly. No threats of ropes or chains? None of this made sense. Finally, he stopped before a door and waited for a nearby servant to open it. Striding inside, he lowered her to her feet near the bed.

And when she needed her leg to be steady, it failed her once more, the muscles in her damaged thigh spasming and sending stabbing pains along the length of it. She clutched at it as she sank to the floor, not able to hide it from either Dougal or the servant who trailed them into the chamber.

'Bloody Symon!' he said through clenched teeth as he reached her side. 'What did he do to you?' The man began to take hold of her skirts, but she pushed him off. No one would see her leg. No one.

'Nay!' she cried as she struggled to drag herself out of his grasp. 'It cramped from...' Lilidh could not think of the excuse so she just waved him off, settling the layers of undergown, gown and tunic as close to her ankles as she could. So she used the truth. 'It cramped.'

Dougal stood back and examined her from head to toe then. Crossing his arms over his broad chest, the man shrugged.

'You can't deny your head is injured. Anything else broken or bleeding?'

Only her heart...

Pushing away that soft thought, she considered all the pain that flooded her body.

'Bumps and bruises, I think,' she said, glancing up at him. 'You are Rob's man, then?' she asked.

'Here now,' Dougal said as he ignored her question and reached down to her, 'take my hand and let's get you to your feet.' Luckily, his hand and arm were much stronger than hers, for if she'd had to rely on hers, she would have remained on the floor. With one fluid movement, he eased her to stand, but did not let go of his hold. 'There you go.'

Lilidh clenched her own jaws now to keep from screaming at the pain that burned through her leg. Closing her fingers into fists, she fought the urge to cry out and to collapse. Weakness was not an option right now. Not when she was a prisoner, when threatened with harm and shame, and when even her presence here would bring the war she'd thought she could stop.

What a fool she was!

First for thinking she could fight off the seasoned warriors who'd captured her. And second, for thinking she could ever make things better between her father and Rob. Third and worst of all, for thinking that seeing him now after everything they'd shared and lost would be less painful than the last time.

Dougal pulled a large wooden chair over towards her and motioned for her to sit on its broad surface. Taking in a breath against the pain and fear of falling, Lilidh moved slowly across the chamber until she reached the chair and lowered herself into it. Closing her eyes, she waited for him to follow his laird's orders to tie or chain her there. A few moments passed before she dared a peek and found him standing with a hand outstretched in front of her...holding out a cup of... something.

'Drink this,' he said, shoving it closer to her. Lilidh dared a sniff, but could smell nothing but the spices used to flavour the wine. She took the cup and brought it to her lips. 'It will ease your pain while Beathas treats your head.'

The woman who'd opened the door for them had been standing by that door all this time and Lilidh never realised it. The pain in her head was dulling her reactions and her senses and kept her from coming up with a plan now that she knew who her attackers were. Once her head stopped throbbing and bleeding, she would be able to think clearly, but first she must ask a question.

'What about my guards? My maid? Who sees to them?' she asked, worrying, too, over those who saw to her care and who she'd last seen lying lifelessly by the side of the road. A shiver raced through her as she asked.

The Matheson man shrugged.

'The laird ordered me to see to you. He will send someone to see to them.'

Understanding it was all she would get as assurances about her people, Lilidh drank down the contents of the cup. From the pungent smell and familiar taste, she suspected that it was a sleeping potion or something to dull the pain in her head. Right at this moment, she hoped it was exactly that. She held out the cup and the woman stepped forwards to take it. It did not take long for the room to change before her eyes.

She noticed that the flames in the hearth, a rather large hearth for a single chamber, swayed this way and that, and she moved her head in time with them. Voices whispered around her, but she could not discern a single clear word in all of the hushed noise. Lilidh lifted her head and turned towards the door and the whole room swirled around her now. Laughing, she enjoyed the warmth that spread into her blood.

Then the door opened, crashing back against the wall, and Rob stood there.

Memories filled her thoughts—of him as a young boy, playing with her brother, learning to work with weapons, growing older and stronger.

Their first kiss.

Lilidh trembled, remembering the gentle, playful touch of their mouths, innocent of anything more. Meeting his intense gaze now, she remembered their growing passion, their secret embraces and the way his scandalous touch would drive her to madness. Then she remembered the way his gaze had hardened when he gave her the truth that broke her heart.

His blue eyes did not sparkle now with the teasing merriment that had tempted her to leave good behaviour behind. Now, anger filled them and another shiver racked her body. With the wine making her feel strange and draining any fear she might have had of him, she stood on unstable legs to meet him and his outrageous claim straight on.

'I will not be your mistress,' she said loudly. The words echoed both inside her head and around it.

She watched as he ordered Dougal and the woman out of the room with a silent tilt of his head. When the door closed and the latch dropped, both making more noise than she'd ever noticed before, she knew it was time.

'I will not make this easy for you, Rob.'

Whatever she expected of him, the quiet laugh was not it, nor the sad smile that curved his lips ever so slightly and made her want to kiss them. Covering her own mouth against the tingling in her lips, she waited. If only she had not drunk the wine, she might be able to talk him out of this.

'No, Lilidh, you never do make things easy for me.'

He took one slow step towards her and then another. She tried to back away, but the chair behind her kept her in place. When he took her by the shoulders and led her to the bed, she should have screamed, but there was no fight left in her.

She was close to collapse, any fool with eyes could see that, both from the potion given by Beathas and her mistreatment at Symon's and his cronies' hands. Her body surrendered to his grasp and he guided her to the bed. Leaning over, Rob scooped her up and laid her there. Though he'd dreamt and hoped for such a thing, this was neither the time nor the manner in which he'd wanted those dreams and hopes to play out.

Lilidh sank into sleep almost as her head touched the pillow and that made it somewhat easier on him. Rob touched her cheek and she did not stir. He gathered her hair, the colour of midnight, and moved it from her face, smoothing it away and searching for any other injuries there.

'She is a feisty one,' Dougal said quietly from his place at the now-open door. Rob nodded and then stepped aside, motioning for both Dougal and Beathas to return to the chamber.

'She has been called that and many other things,' he admitted, though not speaking the ones he'd used the most to describe her. 'See to her injuries, Beathas. All of them.'

His blood heated in anger at the thought of what Symon and his men might have done to Lilidh since they'd taken her from her guards. He should have word on those guards soon, but for now, all he could do was try to make her comfortable before all hell broke loose around them. Again.

The older woman nodded, gathered her supplies together and placed them on the bed. Then she met his gaze and stared at him. The message was clear to him—leave. So, he turned to do so, taking Dougal with him and deciding to set two guards at the door to keep everyone out. As they reached the door, though, he stumbled over a pile of chains, with a number of locks strewn among them. Long sections of heavy rope lay next to the chains.

'Truly, Dougal? Of all the times to obey my orders, you chose this one?' He'd spoken of chains and ropes merely as a public threat, never intending to need them.

'One never knows when a good, stout length of rope or chains might come in handy dealing with a wench such as her,' Dougal said, respect flowing with the words he spoke. Respect for the unconscious woman on his bed. The irony did not escape him in that moment.

'Since the potion will keep her asleep for hours, I need to see to Symon and his cronies. No ropes or chains will be necessary here,' he said. At Dougal's raised brow, he continued, 'For now.'

Chapter Four

'You cannot succeed in this.'

Symon merely laughed at his words as Rob entered the small chamber and closed the door behind him. No matter Symon's attempts to goad him in front of everyone, his reaction at this time would be handled in private. There would always be time to take action against him before the clan later.

'You have as much or more to lose than I do, Symon,' he warned, walking quietly to the window and looking out at the frenzy of activity that his cousin's actions had caused.

'You are a disgrace to the clan,' Symon spat out in a fierce whisper. Turning to face his cousin, the frank hatred in the man's eyes surprised him. 'They should not have chosen you.'

'But they did. And I am not the first bastard

chosen as chieftain of a clan before, Symon. If you would look past your own insulted consequence to the good of the clan—' He had not even finished the words before Symon shook his head.

'I should be chief and laird. I have a claim stronger than yours,' he argued.

'Stronger than blood?' he asked.

Illegitimate or not, his father had been chief and laird here and Symon's claim through his mother to their common grandfather had not been strong enough to cast Rob aside in his favour. Hence the ongoing defiance and now this frank stupidity. His words struck something in Symon, for his cousin's gaze narrowed and he glanced away.

'If my father's wife had delivered a son in a few months, neither of us would be questioning our positions here,' he offered, waiting and watching for any indication of his cousin's involvement in the recent accident that claimed Angus Matheson and his heavily pregnant new wife.

'Aye, but she will not, will she?' Symon asked, neither the expression in his eyes nor the way he held himself betraying anything more.

'You will stand in the same position now as

you would have in that—cousin and adviser to the next laird.'

The elders had already given their support to a betrothal of Rob and Symon's sister so that the fighting between the two branches of the clan could be settled and to strengthen the connections between all of them. Though Rob had his own doubts and reservations about it, it did seem the perfect answer to the problems brought about by Symon's claims. Symon's blood, through his sister's sons, would rule the clan and he would be a valued adviser to the next laird. Symon's gaze darkened, but his tongue remained silent. Rob wondered if his cousin had realised how those arrangements would be muddied and troubled now with the presence of Lilidh MacLerie.

'My sister will not abide you taking the MacLerie's daughter to your bed,' Symon warned.

Rob raised one edge of his brow and smiled. 'Something you should have thought about before bringing her here. I'm certain Tyra understands the way of things among men.'

Men, especially men in power, had women to serve their needs. Wives provided heirs, but no one, no one, would question Rob's right to treat

Lilidh however he wished. If this was to be war, hostages and their treatment were controlled by the chief. Since Symon had delivered her into his hands, he could blame none but himself if his sister was now unhappy over the situation. Symon swallowed deeply and would not meet his gaze. Rob nodded once more.

'I have given you much freedom in speaking your mind here, Symon. But that comes to an end now. You have pushed me and our clan into circumstances that could prove our demise. If you continue to interfere and do not follow my orders, I will outlaw you.' Symon turned swiftly and faced him, his fists clenching and releasing at a furious pace.

'You cannot!'

'The elders approved me as laird. *I* can. I will if you push this,' Rob promised. 'If you cannot console yourself with the place of honour and value you have here, you will be forced out. Doubt it, doubt me, not.'

Symon looked as though he would argue, but at the last moment, he nodded and began to leave. Rob thought it best to add one more item for Symon to consider as he ruminated over his choices and his actions.

'I will not take the sister of a traitor as my wife, Symon, even if the elders believe it will heal the breach between our two lines. I will not marry her if you cannot be loyal. So think long and hard before your words or your actions continue to declare you as such.'

The door slammed without another word being spoken, but as it bounced back open, he watched Symon stride away down the length of the hall. Instead of seeking out his cronies, he waved them off and left the keep.

Since he never doubted that Connor would arrive at his gates due to Symon's actions, he had many things to see to now. All of the clan elders and counsellors would be arriving at his call. When given the true accounting of what Connor could bring against them, Rob felt certain they would understand their precarious position and want to end it quickly. The threat to the clan, their meagre lands and keep included, should be enough to warn them off this dangerous path.

Several tasks had called to him at the same time, so he saw to those and waited on word about Lilidh's servant and guards. If they were alive and she kept unharmed, it could alleviate the MacLerie's legendary temper before he massacred every Matheson there. As he walked from the chamber, the irony struck him.

He would be unworthy of being chieftain if he simply capitulated and released Lilidh to her father and husband.

Though for all the wrong reasons, her presence here gave him an opportunity to improve his family's conditions. With her as a bargaining tool, he could make things better for the Mathesons. Of course, it would mean cementing her hatred of him for ever—though he doubted she felt little else for him even now—and it would be the last time he would see her or speak to her.

And though kidnapping an heiress was a time-honoured tradition here in the Highlands, taking a chief's daughter who happened to be another man's wife did not usually get the same results. With one, a man could end up wealthier with his clan well supported. With the other, wars, death, humiliation, mayhem and possibly beheading or castration followed. Now, since the first was not an issue, he needed to find a way to not allow the latter to happen.

* * *

By the time Rob made his way back up to his chambers that night, several things had fallen into place. Symon seemed cowed for the moment. Only two of Lilidh's guards had died and, though he'd not told her yet, her old serving woman would recover. Beathas reported that the only injuries Lilidh had suffered were the obvious ones and those would heal.

However, the problems that Lilidh caused had not gone away and would increase with every passing hour that she remained in his keep. Until she was healed and he could get to the bottom of this mess, he must hold her and hold her close—for her protection as much as his own.

Walking down the corridor to his chambers, he nodded to the two guards there and sent them off with a wave of his hand. Rob had already set an order for guards to be in place there whenever he wasn't in his room, so he knew they would be back at dawn. Lifting the latch, he stepped inside, ready, he thought, for anything.

The sight before him made the very floor beneath his feet shift.

Lilidh lay on his bed, her hair spread like a

wild, dark storm on the pillows. Her face, washed of grime and dirt, showed the delicate curve of her chin and the pale pink of her lips revealed itself. The potential in her as a child and young girl had blossomed to full beauty as she'd reached womanhood. Beathas had washed her and given her a clean gown. Asleep in his bed, without the fear or pain or anger that had controlled her expression earlier, he could have believed she belonged there.

And from the way his heart thundered in his chest and his blood heated his veins, the sight of her there was something he wanted. Rob nodded to Beathas, who sat by the bed watching over her charge. She put down the garment she worked on and came to him, putting her finger to her mouth, warning him to silence.

'She has just now quieted,' Beathas whispered.

'The potion did not keep her asleep, then?' He glanced across the chamber to watch the slow, calm rise and fall of her chest under the sheet.

'It worked while I had need of it,' Beathas replied.

While the healer tended to the worst of her injuries.

Rob walked closer to the bed. 'Any instructions?'

'Ha,' Beathas grunted out. 'You plan to care for her?' she asked from just behind him.

He'd not really planned this, not really thought beyond Beathas seeing to her injuries. The bold boast he'd made about taking her to his bed muddied things now. Surely no one would expect him to ravish her while unconscious from a head wound?

'I can see to her.' If she planned to argue, she changed her mind then.

'A wee bit of this,' she said, reaching over to the table and lifting a small glass bottle. 'Add it to water or ale and it will help the pain in her head. No' too much, though.'

'Will she sleep now?' Rob asked. He leaned down and smoothed the blanket over Lilidh.

'Nay. Too much sleep when the head is injured is no' a good thing, Rob. If she wakes, let her. If she sleeps, rouse her every few hours and make her speak to you. The potion is only for pain.'

He dismissed her with a wave of his hand. 'I will summon you if I have need of anything else.'

Rob did not turn to see if the older woman

obeyed. Though he expected an argument, none came. Her shuffling feet scuffed over the wood floor as she left. When silence filled the chamber, he let his guard down for a brief moment, running his hands through his hair and letting out a deep breath.

How had his life gone from tolerable to hell in a matter of a few days? How had his position as chief and laird, one he never expected to hold, passed from unquestioned to strongly challenged? Worse, how would he keep his promises to his clan and violate those he'd made years before about Lilidh? Her presence here, and in his bed, broke oaths sworn to her father.

Walking to the table, he poured a cup of ale and sat by the fire, watching her sleep. All of his hopes and fears, all of his aspirations and desires, had once centred on the woman now in his bed. He'd allowed himself to dream of having her as his wife and at his side. He'd believed he could be worthy of her and that her father would accept, even support the match. The truth of it, so far from the dream, had torn them apart years ago.

Was this the fates laughing at him? Did the Almighty have a keen sense of humour after all?

Chuckling over the strangeness of it and trying to figure out a path through the quagmire before him, them, he only then noticed her eyes were open.

'Lilidh,' he said in a hoarse whisper, 'how do you fare now?' When he began to stand, her expression turned to fear, like a wild animal with no place to run. Hating the sight of it, he rested back on the wooden seat.

She began to push herself up as though to move as far from him as possible, but the wincing expression told him of her pain. Then she stopped and closed her eyes, gasping with each movement, no matter how slight.

'Here...' Rob jumped to his feet and strode over to her then. He reached over, grabbed the bottle left by Beathas and poured some of it in the cup of ale there. 'Try sipping this. It will lessen the pain.'

With shaking hands she lifted the cup to her lips and took a small swallow of its contents, grimacing as the bitter liquid trickled into her mouth. Beathas's concoctions, though effective, were known for being nearly undrinkable. Even ale or wine could not cover the less-than-savoury ingredients she used. Rob had not relinquished the cup to Lilidh's control, so he lifted it once then twice and again before taking it from her. That should be enough.

'So, is it time then?' she asked softly, leaning her head back against the wooden headboard.

'For someone who held on to her virtue so tightly for so long, you seem very ready to have your honour taken from you now. Has marriage done that to you?'

He regretted that last barb as it left his lips. Speaking of her marriage to another man was not a topic he wished to think about, let alone discuss with her as she lay in his bed, awaiting ravishment. Rob turned from her, forestalling any reply she might make, and began to put out the candles and bank the remaining flames in the hearth for the night. The inscrutable expression in her eyes when he at last turned back to face her confused him even more.

Did she really expect that he would force himself on her? He knew their parting had been a bad one—he'd shamed her before her family and left her to face their wrath—but never had he forced her. Seduced, cajoled, even begged, but never against her will or without her permission. Had Symon now convinced her that she would pay that price so thoroughly that she accepted it as unavoidable? Shaking his head, overwhelmed by the day's events and confrontations, Rob walked to the last candle at the bedside table and nodded to her.

'Lie down.'

Lilidh's eyes glazed over a bit now as the concoction began its work. Soon, she would once again be in sleep's grasp and he would have time to consider his actions and plans without her interference. He laughed roughly then, which caused her eyes to widen in fear once more. But she followed his order and slid back down under the covers.

After watching until her eyes drifted shut, he put out the last candle, loosened his belt and allowed his plaid to drop to the floor. His boots and shirt went next before he gathered up the length of plaid, climbed on to the bed and covered himself with it. Stretching out, he crossed his arms behind his head and listened to the pattern of her breaths. Soon, without a word more spoken between them, it grew even and deep, signalling her descent into sleep.

He must assert himself on the morrow and bring a calm, reasoned approach to this. He must divorce himself from acting on his feelings of anger and mistrust and lead the clan. He must let go of his past with Lilidh and handle her with detachment and logic. Closing his eyes, he repeated those decisions over and over to himself as he drifted to sleep.

And he might have succeeded had she not whispered a word that put all his thought of control and rationality aside. One whispered word and jealousy and possessiveness and all the long-ago hurt and knowledge of his unworthiness reared within him.

'Iain,' she whispered.

One name. With that one name spoken on a breathless sigh, she ruined all his hopes and once again reminded him of the fruitlessness of his dreams.

Chapter Five

Warmth surrounded her.

Lilidh snuggled deeper beneath the bedcovers, allowing the heat to soothe her sore body. She had found this part of her husband's attentions quite pleasant, for she hated nothing more than waking in a cold chamber with cold feet. As she moved closer to his warm body, a masculine groan filled the space between them.

A groan that did not belong to Iain.

Dear God in Heaven! How could she have forgotten the events of the last days? Forcing her eyes to open even against the glare of what had to be the morning's strong light, Lilidh looked directly into Rob's gaze.

'You are not Iain!' she blurted out as she sought to escape Rob's scandalous embrace. The bedcovers hampered her efforts to scoot back and away from him. The pain that slammed through her head forced her to cease, too, for it threatened to immobilise her with the sheer torture of it. Her stomach rolled from it.

Rob lifted the arm that had most recently crossed her breasts and leaned up on his side. Covered only with his plaid, one that had carelessly been tossed over him from the look of it, he watched her without saying a word. Unlike Iain who simply rolled out of their bed and left their chamber each morn without saying anything, Rob clearly had other plans.

'No, not Iain,' he whispered in a voice so deep it made her feel as though heated honey was running over and through her body.

He looked dishevelled from sleep. A lock of his hair kept falling into his eyes. Lilidh reached out to move it away, stopping herself only at the last moment. Damn him! How dare he order her kidnapped and brought here like this. Fool that she always was when it came to him, she wanted to help smooth out the tensions between him and her father. Rob blinked then, turning his gaze from hers as he lifted the plaid and slid to the edge of the bed.

His bed.

She swallowed. Try as she might, she could not look away as his strong, muscular back was exposed to her, all the way to his... Tanned from exposure to the sun, the muscles rippled as he bent down and reached for something on the floor. Her mouth went dry as he tugged a shirt over his head and stood as its length fell around him.

Though it covered his back, it did not reach much lower than his thighs, so his legs, just as well defined as his back, were open to her sight. He'd grown and filled out from the last time she spied on her brother and him as they swam naked in a lake near her home. The passing years, along with the fighting and training, had added bulk and strength to his body. When he faced her, boots and plaid in hand, their gazes met and only the slight lifting of one corner of his mouth gave her any indication of his reaction to her blatant perusal of him.

'Do I look like Iain?' he asked, picking up his boots.

He must never have met Iain or he would not ask the question. Two men could never have looked so differently as he and Iain—had. Iain was nearly two-score-and-ten and his hair had long gone grey. He had retained his warrior's stature and strength even until his death. Then Lilidh remembered that the MacGregors were attempting to keep the news of his death from spreading too far while they settled the dispute over his heir and successor.

As happened whenever she thought of her now-dead husband, confusion and regret entered her heart and mind. He had seemed healthy and stout as long as she'd known him, so his sudden and unexpected death, and their short marriage, left more questions and fears in their passing than they answered.

'No, not alike at all,' she finally forced out so that he would not stare so intently at her. Turning away, she reached up to examine her head and the bandage she felt there. Truly, she just could not meet his gaze or think about Iain and her failure to please him at this moment. Not when every-thing was out of control. 'Did you…?'

He frowned for a moment and then his gaze darkened. 'Did I what?'

Lilidh could not speak the words. She did not

know if he could have had his way with her while she'd been unconscious or not. That place between her legs felt no worse or different than it ever had, so she had not a clue whether he'd taken her or not. The fog caused by the strong medicine in the healer's brew hid any memory of the last day and night. He waited for an answer, so she glanced down at the bed and then back at him.

A sudden and terrible thought occurred to her in that moment of waiting—what if her virgin's blood marked his sheets and exposed her shame and the failure of her marriage? Would he use it to further his clan's aim to bring dishonour and humiliation to her and her father? Questions would be raised about the validity of her marriage to the MacGregor chief and the treaties attached to it if anyone knew it had never been consummated.

And now there was no way to look without drawing his attention. So, Lilidh waited for him to speak. She swallowed against the fear of exposure and shame and waited for him to answer— too afraid to look and too afraid to look away.

'Lilidh,' he said in a quiet voice. 'Look at me.'

She did not allow the soft tone to mislead her into thinking it was less than a direct command.

She took in a deep breath, tried to keep from trembling and did as he'd ordered. Instead of the mocking she thought to find there, Lilidh watched as desire filled those blue eyes. Desire so strong she felt it pulse through her as though he touched her everywhere at once. Her skin heated, her blood raced and her mouth went dry.

'When I take you to my bed, in my bed, you will remember it. You will remember every caress, every kiss, when it happens.'

Lilidh felt every word he said and the memories of their time together and this promise of what would come between them shot through her body as if he *had* touched her. And in those words were every sensation she'd hope to feel and to experience with her husband, but had not. Hearing Rob say them, she mourned for the thousandth time their regrettable ending with its harsh words. Her skin tingled and her blood heated, waiting as desire burned a path through her.

Then, the flare of passion she'd seen there was over and gone. The fire she'd witnessed turned to cold, icy blue and he walked away without another word. Lilidh watched as he lifted the bar off the door and placed it on the floor and then reached for the latch.

'Do not attempt to leave this room or speak to anyone save Beathas and Dougal.'

'I have questions,' she said before he could leave. Rob glanced back then and shook his head at her.

'And I have duties to see to,' he replied as he opened the door.

He spoke quietly to whoever waited there and then he was gone. Though she knew others were just outside the door, no one entered. Lilidh tested her limbs, stretching them as best she could, and then pushed herself slowly to the edge of the bed. Sliding from its height, she grabbed hold of the bedpost and stood, letting her body and her head adjust for a few minutes.

When her legs steadied beneath her, she held her breath, pushed her hair back over her shoulders and took a cautious step. Then, letting go of her support, another and another until she reached the chair by the now-cold hearth. Grabbing for the back of that chair, she wobbled a bit and then used it to edge around until she could sit.

Taking in deep breaths against the pain in her head and the tightness of every part of her, she closed her eyes and tried to think of more pleasant things. It had always helped her in the past and she prayed it would now. Clenching the sides of the chair, she fought off the desire to cry out from the torment.

'Here now, dearie…'

The words and approach of a woman broke into her thoughts and she gasped in surprise more than anything else. Beathas, the healer, had returned. Carrying linens under her ancient arm and a large chamberpot in her hands, the woman bobbed from side to side in a most worrying way. Without thought, Lilidh stood to help her. The pain took her breath away with its severity.

'Poor wee lass,' Beathas whispered as she put the supplies down and came to her side. Easing Lilidh back to the chair, she cooed and offered warm, comforting nonsensical words, at once becoming the caregiver. 'Would you no' be more comfortable in the bed for a wee bit?'

Lilidh closed her eyes, unable to speak and

torn between the pain and the gentle care of this stranger. The woman did not push her to move. Instead, taking up a brush, she eased Lilidh's hair back and began slow, long strokes away from the injured place. When she closed her eyes and blocked out her surroundings, she could have believed herself home, being tended by her mother. She may have even fallen to sleep for a moment, so comforting were the motions of the brush, followed by Beathas's tender touch as she tamed Lilidh's tangled hair while avoiding the bandaged, injured area.

'Do you have a looking glass?' she asked the woman. Her skin was easily marked by bruises or bumps and Lilidh wondered how badly she must look after the last days of rough handling by the one who brought her here and his cronies.

'I don't, my lady,' Beathas said. 'I will see if Tyra has one in her chambers that you could use.'

'Tyra?' An unfamiliar name, but then she had not kept track of Rob's clan in years.

'Symon's sister,' Beathas explained. A hesitation in her reply spoke of much information not to be shared.

'Never you mind, then,' Lilidh said. 'I do not wish you to be drawn into this.'

'Did he hurt you, dearie?'

The question was slipped in quietly, but confused Lilidh for she did not know if Beathas referred to Symon or Rob. Whichever it was, she had no intention or desire to speak of such things, for it would bring up other personal matters.

'Leave it be, Beathas. I know that I am prisoner and enemy and do not expect to be treated otherwise while here,' she said with far more confidence than she felt.

It was the truth, though, and an attitude she feared she must accept to get through this ordeal. If things had deteriorated so much that Rob's clan thought kidnapping her and shaming her father was the correct course of action, then she could not be certain of anything—least of all how she would indeed be treated. As laird and chief, Rob would have to appease his clan elders and those whose backing he needed to remain on the high chair. Forcing her to his bed, beating her or shaming her could all be part of it.

A shiver racked her then. She was a woman alone—no guards, no family, no husband—with no one to watch over her and protect her. Had her father received word yet about her kidnapping? Had Rob or that rogue Symon sent demands? If no one was left alive from her travelling group, who would take the news to her father or to the MacGregors?

The tears surprised her then, coming without warning at the thought of her friends and family lying dead by the road after the attack. Poor Isla! Her faithful maid had been with her for years, first as her nurse, then companion as she grew older and did not need a nurse. Accompanying her on her marriage journey to Iain's clan gave Lilidh comfort, as her mother had said it would. Any number of cousins could have come with her, but her mother had advised only Isla until Lilidh had settled in.

Now, she was responsible for the woman's death and the death of others who had simply carried out their orders.

Leaning her head down, she let the tears flow. Her body rocked slightly on its own as sorrow filled her heart and soul at the loss of so many. The healer's gentle touch on her shoulder surprised her.

'Here now,' Beathas whispered. 'All will be well.'

The woman wrapped a blanket around her shoulders and tucked it tightly. She moved quietly around the chamber, straightening the bed and cleaning as she went. Every so often a soft tsking would be heard, but the woman did not ask her any other questions. Lilidh gathered her emotions under control and let the temporary sadness and tears go. For now.

For now she needed to be strong. To be the daughter of the MacLerie and the widow of the proud MacGregor chieftain. To survive this coming ordeal she must keep her wits and find out what Rob's plans were—especially with her. And she must find ways to influence Rob's decisions, if possible, too.

For years she'd observed her uncle negotiating and watched her father be both the *Beast* and the wise leader. This was the time to use everything she'd learned to save herself, her honour and possibly save the man she'd wanted to marry all those years ago. Taking a deep breath, she loosened the blanket and pushed it down. She must be ready to face him on his return.

'I would like to wash, if that's permitted,' she said quietly without looking at Beathas. Without a word, Beathas went to the door, opened it and whispered to whoever stood guard there.

'Some hot water will be here for you soon. And something warm to drink as well, lass.'

Lilidh sat in the quiet, waiting for those things and trying to see a pattern in what Symon had said while taunting her and in what Rob had said in the hall, snatches of which came drifting back to her now as she thought about it. For certain, she'd been taken because of her father, though little had been said about her connection to Iain and the MacGregors. Only muffled curses and a few words had been directed at her after they'd tied, gagged and hooded her and brought her here.

She thought that Symon might have initiated this action in trying to force Rob's hand. If she'd been coherent and uninjured during her taking, she might have learned more. Now, as a loud knock startled her from her thoughts, she would have to wait.

Beathas answered it, opening the door widely to allow entrance to whoever waited. A large wooden tub was rolled in and placed to one side of the chamber. Men followed, carrying buckets of steaming water. A woman entered with a pile of linens and handed them to Beathas. Lilidh watched out the corner of her eye, having no desire to meet what she was sure would be the curious gazes of these Mathesons.

Once the room had emptied and Beathas had arranged things as she wanted them to be, Lilidh pushed herself out of the chair and stood. She could not stop the groan of pain as her body fought her efforts to move. A warm cup was pressed into her hands before she knew it.

'Betony tea. To soothe the hurts and ease your moving around.'

Deciding she could not sort things out and accomplish anything until she was recovered, Lilidh sipped from the cup and discovered the tea was sweetened and flavourful. She drank a bit and then handed it back to Beathas.

'I will finish it after I wash,' she said, limping to the side of the tub. Reaching down, she swirled her fingers in the water and found it to be steaming hot—perfect for a long soak. 'I can see to this myself.'

The expected argument from the old woman

did not happen. Beathas moved a short stool close to the tub and placed the drying linens and a small bowl of soap on it.

'Summon me if you wish help with your hair,' Beathas said as she walked to the door. 'Have a care for the wound.'

If there had been a way to lock or bar the door, Lilidh would have. Seeing none, she steadied herself and dropped the blanket from her shoulders. She gathered up the length of the shift she wore and pulled it over her head, dropping it to the floor where it would remain dry. Shaking her head, she glanced around the chamber for her gown and did not see it. Had Beathas taken it?

No matter, she thought, grasping the side of the tub and easing her stronger leg over the side. Once on the bottom of it, she pulled her bad leg into the water. Using the sides of the tub, she slid slowly down until she sat. It was large enough for her to stretch out her legs and she moaned as the hot water surrounded her tight muscles and the scars. Other than walking, a hot bath did much to loosen the tightness when the cramping came upon her. After the last several days, this was nigh to heaven, so she leaned back and let the heat seep into her.

Though used to Isla's gentle ministrations during her baths, Lilidh managed to scrub the dirt from her legs and arms and even wash her hair, though she thought she might spill more water from the tub than she left in it. Once done, she soaked in the water until it lost its heat. Having a care not to slip, she climbed from the water, wrapped her hair in a cloth and then used another to dry off the rest of her. She'd just claimed the warm, woolen blanket again, clutching it around the once again worn shift, when the door opened.

'The laird has called for your presence down in the hall,' Beathas said. She placed the bundle of clothing she carried on the bed and reached up to help with Lilidh's hair. 'I will plait it for you for now. He was clear that you not delay.'

From the frown on Beathas's face and her lack of encouragement, Lilidh knew this could not be a good thing. Feeling more revived from the bath, she allowed Beathas to help her dress in the plain gown, stockings and shoes she'd brought. Once done, she tried to fortify herself for whatever would come. When the door opened and Rob's man stood waiting with a rope, Lilidh was not certain she would ever be ready.

Chapter Six

Symon strode through the hall towards the tower where his and Tyra's chambers were. Climbing the stairs and reaching her rooms, he knocked and lifted the latch without waiting for a response. Angered at the path his plans had taken, he would not be left standing in the corridor waiting like some fool. His sister glared at him, but said nothing. With a nod of his head, the two maids helping her dress fled. Tyra turned back to her looking glass and arranged a ribbon that drooped loosely down her cheek.

Women! Damn them all!

Symon crossed the chamber in a few strides and yanked the ribbon free, causing several locks of Tyra's hair to fall as well. He tossed the ribbon in her face and crossed his arms. Instead of looking fearful or giving him the respect he deserved from her, she just smiled, selected another strip of material from her collections and wove her hair back in place. All without a word to him! Just when his fist itched to teach her her rightful place, she spoke.

'So what is my betrothed's new mistress like, Symon?'

'Mistress? Give her not some title as exalted as mistress, Tyra. She is nothing but a MacLerie whore warming his bed.'

'Only that, then?' she replied. Symon's own brow twitched as Tyra raised one of hers in question. 'Only a woman in his bed?'

'You know the way of things, Sister. He will use her until her father gives in to our demands and then she will be gone from here.'

'Was that your plan? When you brought her here?' Her voice was so calm it gave him pause. Instead of screaming at him as her usual custom would be, she had not raised her voice or seemed angered by what he'd done.

'My plan was to keep her as my captive, in my bed, until her father paid for her release,' Symon admitted.

The sight of Lilidh MacLerie riding along the

forest road had aroused him. He'd planned on claiming her body and using it as he wished when she was his to command. Then her daring actions, fighting his men and trying to protect the old woman, heated his blood and his lust for her almost overpowered him. Oh, aye, she would be good for some bold bedplay. Even now his body readied to take hers. Only his sister's cough brought his attention back to their conversation.

'Now she is Rob's plaything to bed and use. I am not happy about this, Symon.' Tyra stood, smoothing her gown down as she stepped closer to him. Leaning in, she whispered to him, 'Take her back, Symon. Get her out of his bed.'

Symon almost took a step back at the vehemence in her tone. Almost. But he was the man here and, though Tyra was his elder sister, he would not take orders from a woman.

'You will listen to me, Tyra,' he commanded in a low voice. There was no need for servants and the like to overhear this conversation. 'She is a temporary stone in the path here. A means to an end. Once we have the gold from the MacLerie, she will be gone and we will be richer. And I will be able to take the chieftain's chair

from the bastard. Our plans will all see success.'
She made to step around him, but he grabbed her
arm to stop her.

'I will be laird here, so you had better watch
your step and do as I tell you to do. I will not be
as pliable as that whoreson Rob is when it comes
to giving you your way if you disobey me in this.'

Something flickered in her eyes for a moment
before she masked it. Something he could not
identify. Something dead.

'But, of course, Brother,' she replied, bowing
her head. 'I value your guidance in all things.'

He huffed out a breath and released her. As
long as she realised that she was beholden to him
for her position, things would work out. Symon
lifted the latch and pulled on the door before
glancing back at Tyra. Her expression was one
of humility and obedience, but that was not what
he'd seen there before.

Not at all.

Tyra kept her gaze blank until Symon left her
chambers and then her anger filled her. Clenching her fists, she searched for something, anything, to throw and break. The need to smash

something into the floor or wall grew uncontrollable and she finally spied just the thing—her looking glass.

A present from her stepfather, Symon's father, she took the heavy metal object with both hands and flung it to the floor, sending pieces off in different directions across the chamber. The larger reflecting piece skidded satisfyingly on the rough wood until it slammed into the wall.

Tyra seethed with rage. Men always controlled her life. Her father, then her stepfather, her brother and now the newly made laird who had agreed to take her as wife. Agreed, aye, after having to be convinced by the worthless elders! Yet now he felt no shame or hesitation in sleeping with another woman before all of them. No explanation to her, no words to soften the blow to her pride. She was simply expected to accept this treatment as her place in life and be grateful for it.

Grateful was not something that she did easily or well.

Damn that fool Symon! This move had cost much and confounded her own plans. If he had only left well enough alone and let those elders who agreed with him push Rob out, all would have been well and her future would have been as she'd desired. Now, Rob was exerting his own pressures on the elders and the rest and the MacKenzies seemed less and less appealing as allies in the face of the MacLerie's forces.

Damn him!

The sound of footsteps approaching her door alerted her that she had to regain control of herself. Men might not know how to control themselves, but Tyra would not her plans fail because of excessive emotions. Letting out her breath, she forced her face to relax and cleared her mind of thoughts, until she could allow a smile to alight on her mouth.

'I misjudged its weight,' she said apologetically as she turned to face her serving woman. The woman went scurrying around the bedchamber, gathering up the scattered pieces of metal.

'Oh, my lady,' Margaret whispered, holding out the broken looking glass. ''Tis the one that your stepfather gave you on the anniversary of your birth!'

'Mayhap the smith can repair it? Would you

take it to him and ask him?' she said, smiling at the maid.

'Oh, aye, my lady,' Margaret said, ever trying to please her mistress since she and the others expected her to be the woman who would rule over this household very soon.

Tyra waited for her to leave before sitting down before the table that used to hold the looking glass. She smoothed her hair back and tugged on the sleeves of the gown. She must appear in the hall soon and act as though everything in her life pleased her. As though she was not bothered at all by her betrothed bedding another woman while the entire clan knew. As though she was happy at the thought of becoming lady here. As though this was her perfect life and would be her perfect future.

She had learned long ago how to bide her time; it was a lesson hard-learned and not forgotten. Not then and not now. Everything these fools planned would be for naught and in the end she would rule over the household of her beloved—Gavin MacKenzie, the heir to the vast MacKenzie lands and wealth.

And they would learn that they should never have underestimated her.

Lairig Dubh

Jocelyn did not like it one bit.

Something was going on and no one would tell her what it was. Rurik, usually the one to spill any news first, simply watched her silently. Duncan, the clan's negotiator, came and went from Connor's meetings without meeting her gaze.

Oh, aye, something bad was afoot in the clan MacLerie.

Connor had sent a servant to summon her back from the village, but upon her arrival at Lairig Dubh, he'd kept her waiting. Her patience, nonexistent when she was worrying over her family, wore through at that moment and she climbed to her feet, put her basket on the table and prepared to find out the truth.

'Jocelyn,' Connor said quietly, opening his door to her. 'Come. We must speak.'

All her bluster left her at the look on his face. Bad? This was not bad—this was a disaster of some kind. Jocelyn attempted to smooth her breathing and not lose control as she tried to remember where each of their children was. Where each of Connor's kin was. Where every person she cared about was at that moment. Yet, none of that helped in this tense moment.

Connor took her hand and escorted her into his private chamber as the others left. He led her to a chair, but she shook off his hold and his attempt.

'Just tell me, Connor.' Steeling her heart and nerves, she waited for the news.

'Lilidh has been...' Connor paused, searching for a word while her heart stopped. Dead? Was her daughter dead? She clasped her hands together and held her breath. 'Kidnapped.'

'Kidnapped? She is alive?' Jocelyn sank on to the chair then, unable to keep her legs steady. 'Who did this?'

'Rob Matheson.'

She shook her head. Rob? No, not him. 'That cannot be. You fostered Rob. He was the son of your friend, your ally. He loved...' She paused before saying the rest because she knew it would simply inflame Connor's temper.

'All of that is in the past now,' he growled, turning away from her. 'One of the men escorting her home survived and made his way here, reporting on what had happened. But first he followed the men who took her and they took her to the Matheson keep.'

'None of this makes sense, Connor,' she said, twisting her hands in her lap as she thought of her eldest child. 'Why would he take her? He is betrothed to someone else, so marriage is not his aim. He has no quarrel with you.'

Her words drifted off as she realised that there was no peace between her husband and his foster son. The division between them might have begun because of Lilidh, but recent changes could be blamed on the Mathesons negotiating with their common adversaries, the MacKenzies.

'What will you do?' Her mother's heart beat erratically, worried at all the terrible possibilities and the few good ones in this situation. Connor glanced at her and she held her breath.

'She is a hostage now. Her kidnapping is a prelude to war.'

Her head spun even as her heart raced then and she felt her legs shake beneath her. Connor was at her side in an instant, embracing her in his strong arms.

'Connor, you must—'

She would have offered up all kinds of solutions, all from a mother's caring heart, but her husband, her laird, placed his finger over her lips and shook his head.

'I know all the words you would speak right now, Jocelyn,' he began. 'Remember that she is the daughter of an earl and a chieftain. A widow to the great MacGregor chief. Tied to two of the most powerful families in the Highlands. The Mathesons would be fools to mistreat her.'

At this time.

She heard the words as though he'd spoken them. Their daughter was safe for now, though what *safe* meant could be another complete discussion.

'For now, I am sending a messenger to Rob to ask for his terms.'

'You will not attack?' Her worst fear.

'I can always attack,' he said. The hint of bloodthirst in his voice revealed that the beast was still there and ready to rise when needed. 'First, I will try diplomacy.'

'I would see her,' Jocelyn tried. 'I would accompany Duncan to Keppoch and make certain she is well.' Duncan would be the first choice to handle such a delicate and dangerous matter for Connor.

She pushed out of his embrace, determined to gather some clothing and supplies and be ready to leave. She and other wives had travelled with their husbands and kin on matters of state and clan business and this would be nothing different.

'You will stay here and see to your duties.'

She tensed at the words and the tone in which he delivered them. Turning to face him, Jocelyn saw that he did not jest with her. He expected her to remain here while the fate of her, their, daughter hung in the balance. He expected her to continue to see to her duties and to act as though nothing was wrong. He expected her to...

'Aye, I do, Jocelyn.'

They'd lived and loved so long now that he could indeed read her thoughts, though she considered that it might have been her face and expression that gave her away. She'd never been good at hiding her feelings—not long ago when they met and not now that they'd been married for almost a score of years.

She looked away from him then, trying to hold back the tears and anger that threatened to erupt.

She would be of no help to her husband or their daughter if she fell apart as she wished to do in that moment. Tightening her lips so no words escaped, she thought on how her own goal could be accomplished even in the face of Connor's resistance.

'I think I prefer the devastated mother's expression to the mutinous MacCallum one you wear now,' he observed, crossing his arms over the wide expanse of his chest and glaring at her.

She shrugged and shook her head. 'I know not what you—'

'Come now, Jocelyn. We have been through so much together and I am insulted that you think I do not know what that look in your eyes and the tilt of your chin up ever so slightly…' he said, as he reached out and outlined the curve of her chin and face down to her neck. Chills shot through her at his touch. Any time. Every time. '…means. It means you plan to defy me in this.'

'Connor, surely—' She withheld any further arguments.

'I think I would prefer not to hear a lie from your lips,' he admitted. His stern gaze gave her no sign of leniency, only understanding. However, her husband was an intelligent man who could make the right decisions when left to it. She waited and finally after several seconds heard his exhaled breath. 'Do nothing that will lessen our chances of getting what we need. Pay heed to Duncan and Rurik.'

Duncan *and* Rurik? If he was sending both, he was preparing for war as well and making quite a show of strength. That manoeuvre could either impress the Mathesons or cause them to act rashly. She prayed in that moment that it was the former and not the latter.

'When?'

'We must wait on them and the messengers I've sent before sending armed men to his lands. Give him a chance to come to his damned senses and release her on his own.' He paused then. 'About a sennight, I would think.

'You will do nothing that Duncan and Rurik do not give permission to do while there. You will remain within our camp and—' When he began to announce a long list of orders and prohibitions, she stopped him the one sure way she knew would work—she stood on the tips of her toes and kissed him.

He clasped her shoulders and held her close, their breaths mingling, as he stared into her eyes and studied her face. Then he settled her back to her feet and released her.

'You will be safe, Jocelyn.' She nodded and began to leave, for there was much planning and packing to do. 'And, Jocelyn? I am allowing you to go in case Lilidh needs you,' he explained.

Those last words would haunt her days and nights until she next beheld her daughter and could ascertain for herself any damages done to her at the hands of the Mathesons.

Oh, woe to Rob Matheson if her daughter was harmed. Woe to him if he incurred the wrath of a mother! Connor could not be more dangerous than that.

Chapter Seven

Lilidh was out of breath and straining with each step by the time they reached the lower level where the hall was located. Dougal had gone slowly, but that mattered not right now. The pain in her leg, eased by the long soak in the hot water, was back in full force. Spasms pulsed through her leg with each step. Finally they stopped and Dougal let her catch her breath. When she looked up and met his gaze, she saw pity enter and she hated it.

'Hold out your hands,' he said. Dougal took the length of coiled rope off his shoulder, found the end and tied a looped knot in it.

Her time as a prisoner officially began now and all who saw her would know it.

She reached up and tucked the strands of hair that had come loose from the braid back behind her ears and then offered her hands to him. She needed to stay alive until Rob and her father could sort this out. She needed to remain unharmed or her father would not let a stone remain standing in this keep or village. So, she did not fight this.

When he finished, he let some rope drop between them and began to lead her into the hall. All the talking stopped as she entered and she could feel their scrutiny as she made her way slowly towards the front. To the dais where Rob no doubt sat eating. Along with the scoundrel Symon who'd brought her here. She swallowed back her anger with him, because she must stay in control of herself for now.

Her head pounded with each step. She noticed some of those watching muttered or whispered under their breath. Some looked away and would not meet her eyes. She saw hatred and distrust in some; in most she thought she recognised pity and sympathy. Especially from the women. By the time they walked the length of the big chamber, she was limping badly and out of breath again. But she squared her shoulders when she stopped before him, for she was a MacLerie and would not let them forget it.

'Here she is, Symon,' Rob said loudly enough for all to hear. 'Not too coddled, as you accused.'

A young woman sat between the two men and she realised this must be the Lady Tyra who Beathas had mentioned. Lovely, with long, auburn hair and green eyes and a heart-shaped face, the look in her eyes seared Lilidh with hatred. As quickly as it had appeared, it was gone, and the woman turned her softened gaze towards Rob. Lilidh blinked, thinking that exhaustion had caused her to see something that was not there after all.

'Must she be here at all? Her very presence insults me.'

Bold, this one was, to say such a thing. Lilidh was the equal to any noble-born woman, daughter of an earl, so to hear such a thing surprised her. Prisoner, aye, but a noblewoman none the less. Symon's sister bowed her head—a humbling nod in other circumstances, but one played just for Rob and the others now. Even Lilidh could see it plainly.

'Take her back, Dougal,' Rob called out.

'Hold!' Symon shouted when Dougal took her by the arm. 'She is a prisoner here and should not have a life of leisure while we wait to hear from the MacLerie.'

A few men called out in support of his words with loud, rude words and noises. From the sound of it, they believed she should be performing personal services of a kind she did not wish to think upon. She lifted her face and looked to Rob.

His calm expression surprised her.

He did not look as though he was interested in her at all. He stood then and walked to where Symon stood, ignoring the lady's soft pleas to return to her. Now, watching her speak to Rob, Lilidh suspected that she was more than simply sibling to the brigand. When Rob reached Symon, he pushed his cousin out of the way and took her by the arm, tugging her up on the step.

'Lady Lilidh MacLerie is mine. You brought her here, Symon, and I claim her as chief. For as long as she remains here, she is mine alone. If anyone else touches her, they answer to me.'

Her face must be the colour of her favourite ribbon—scarlet! How could he boldly claim such things when she stood there with them? And making such a claim in front of both Symon and his sister shocked her, but at the same time, it reassured her. His grasp loosened and she stumbled down from the step, regaining her balance once there. She thought him done, until he spoke once more.

'But you are right, Symon. 'Tis wrong for a prisoner to expect to be treated as a guest. When I have no need for her, she will work in the kitchens.'

She could not help it—she gasped at his crude insinuation and his command. Work in the kitchens? She would not. Lilidh began to walk away when she found her path blocked by Dougal. 'I am not your servant,' she said to Rob and she faced him.

'You will do what you are told to do, lady,' Rob ordered as he approached. 'You will do it when you are told to do it. Or I swear that I'll be delivering your dead body to your father once he arrives.'

In spite of not believing he would harm her, the sight of his fists clenching and opening, clenching and opening, made her take a step away. She began to back up until Dougal blocked her path and she could go no further.

Was this was a Rob she'd never known? Unpredictable? Dangerous? Was whatever leniency he'd granted her the day and night before over now and did she face him as an enemy this morn? And she was not only alone, but also very overwhelmed and confused. Unable to stand up to him in strength or power, she did the only prudent thing in this situation.

Lilidh dropped to her knees and bowed her head.

If every foul word she'd ever heard or overheard tried to force its way onto her tongue and out of her mouth, 'twas no fault of hers. Keeping silent at a time like this went against every fibre in her body and soul, but she was no fool. Staying alive to fight another day in another way was her plan. If it required her to swallow all those curses, then so be it.

For now.

Rob grunted from somewhere above her. He grunted! Then Symon seemed to copy the sound. From being raised around so many egotistical, proud, strong men, she recognised it as the sound men made when their pride was satisfied. When she dared to raise her head a bit, she watched as a satisfied smirk found its place on the face of the lovely Lady Tyra. Before she could think more on that, Rob spoke again.

'Dougal, take her to the kitchens. She can begin there now.'

Dougal's strong hands wrapped around her shoulders giving her more help in rising than was apparent to others, but she felt it. Once on her feet, he tugged the rope and led her from the hall. They talked about her as even she left and could still hear them.

'Are you satisfied now, Symon? She will be worked from morning to night in the kitchens and then serve me in my bed,' Rob said.

She so hoped Symon would not speak again, but from her short experiences with the man, she understood he would never give up the chance to have the last word. She prepared herself for something vulgar.

'I am glad that you, at least, followed my advice on how to treat her, Rob. Tame her with a strong hand and keep riding the bitch until she cannot walk. It's all she or her father will understand.'

Fury and pride waged a war within her. How dare they speak of her and of such things about her! Lilidh was about to stop and reply to the lewd words, but Dougal chose to give a real and hard yank on the rope just then and she stumbled forwards, staying on her feet her only thought. Laughter erupted around her. She dared a last glance back as they reached the doorway.

It was a hall divided. Though most of the men laughed, the women sat silently, directing looks of pity in her direction. More than one woman whispered something to her man which caused them to stop laughing. Only one group continued to call out, encouraged on by Symon. His friends, no doubt, and those responsible for capturing her at his side.

Another tug on the rope from Dougal and she shuffled along, limping as she went. If they all chose to believe it was from Rob's treatment of her, she was not about to disabuse them of that notion right now. A prisoner, a hostage, needed to use whatever tools were at her disposal.

They made their way down the back corridors until they reached the kitchen. It bustled with people carrying out tasks to store and prepare food for the clan. Men, women, even boys, moved quickly in and out of the noisy room, all under the direction of an even-louder, huge man who wielded a large wooden spoon like a sword. When he spotted her and Dougal, he shrugged and frowned.

'What is this, Dougal? Are you going through my kitchen to reach the dungeon now?'

The cook. As she thought.

'She's to work here, at the laird's orders, I'm afraid, Calum,' Dougal replied.

'What am I to do with a lady in my kitchen? Did he think about that?' Calum asked with the attitude of a man in charge who did not want interference from anyone. From the tone, she knew he did not expect an answer.

'Here now, Calum,' a woman interrupted. 'I will see to her.' The woman walked to the cook's side and whispered something to him. Her words seemed to calm him, for he nodded several times before speaking.

'Siusan will take her, Dougal.' He motioned her away. 'Any other orders from the laird, then?' She knew not of a cook who appreciated any visitors or disturbances in their kitchen and Lilidh almost smiled at how closely Calum fit the mould.

Dougal shook his head and followed Siusan away from the main area. Still tethered to him, she went, glancing around the hustling place. They stopped before a large table in one far corner.

'Give her to me,' Siusan said, waiting and watching Dougal. When he held out the rope, the woman shook her head. 'What good does a bound servant do me, Dougal? There is no task here that doesn't use her hands.'

The stout woman placed her hands on her hips and stared Dougal down as Lilidh watched. Clearly, it was not something he'd considered on their way here.

'She is a prisoner, Siusan. Not to have the freedom of a guest. Do you understand?'

'Aye, Dougal,' she said in a tired voice. 'We have all heard about the laird's plans for her. Work her here, work her in his bed.' Lilidh blinked quickly, fighting back both a laugh and a retort. News travelled quickly, but even faster through the servants in a keep.

Silently, Dougal untied her hands and coiled the

rope back up and pulled it onto his shoulder. She met his gaze for a moment and knew he was not amused. But, truly, what could he do? Or rather, what did he need to do? With her maimed leg, she would not be running away. In this place filled with Symon's cronies who thought nothing of hurting her, where would she run?

'She is not to be left alone. Someone on guard at all times.' Siusan waved her hands in a sweeping motion, urging him out, so Dougal turned and left.

'So, what can you do in a kitchen?' Siusan asked as she pointed to a stool next to the table.

Grateful to sit after so long on her feet, Lilidh walked slowly to it, held on to the edge of the table and lowered herself on the wooden surface. Looking up, she noticed that Siusan stared at her as she moved. Lilidh was about to answer her question, when the woman spoke first.

'Has Beathas seen to you, lass?' she whispered.

Siusan, like the others, thought Rob had beaten her. Since most had not seen her when she arrived in the hall, wrapped and filthy, it was a natural assumption to make, she supposed. Deciding not to say much about it, Lilidh nodded and looked away.

'My mother made certain I can do most kitchen tasks, though I have little skill at cooking,' she answered the first question instead. 'I was expected to oversee my husband's household,' Lilidh said into the surprised woman's face.

Siusan called one of the rushing-by girls over and took a basket from her. Reaching into her own belt, she pulled out a small paring knife and held it out to Lilidh.

'Clean and chop these,' she directed, as Lilidh took both of them. 'And I'll be having that knife back before you leave here.'

Lilidh smiled and when Siusan did as well, she knew she had not misunderstood the woman's attempt at humour. Oh, there were many things she could do with that knife, but she would not risk it—yet.

She'd cleaned several baskets of vegetables when her stomach reminded her she had not eaten that day. Or even the last one, for all she'd had was Beathas's concoctions. Siusan heard the rumblings as she moved around the table.

'Have you eaten today?' she asked.

'No,' Lilidh replied.

'When last did you eat?' The woman walked closer.

Lilidh shrugged, for she really did not know. If she'd slept through most of one day and into another, and had been on the road for another one with Symon, had it been three days? 'A while.'

Within moments, a large bowl of broth and a chunk of bread were placed before her. A mug at the plate's side. 'Go ahead,' Siusan said.

Though plain, Lilidh thought she'd never tasted anything so good before. She tore the bread into pieces and dipped them in the broth to soften them. Within minutes, she'd eaten every bit and drank down the remaining broth, too. She had not realised how hungry she had been until the first taste of food in her mouth. Smiling at how her brother would tease her over eating so quickly, she looked up to find Siusan studying her.

'My thanks,' she said, gathering the bowl and mug together and pushing herself to stand. If she did not move around, her leg would stiffen beyond measure on her.

'You have her look,' Siusan said as Lilidh carried the bowl over to a large tub used to wash dishes and such.

'Her look?' she asked, not understanding.

'Your mother. I visited a cousin who lives in Lairig Dubh and saw her. The laird's wife.'

'Jocelyn MacCallum?' Lilidh asked.

'Aye, you have her eyes and the shape of her face, though your hair is the colour of your father's.' Siusan smiled then. 'The Beast, they called him…but that was so long ago.'

The woman still stared at her and Lilidh wondered why.

'They still call him that, though not loud enough for him to hear,' Lilidh answered.

'I did not think Rob the kind of man to do that,' she said softly, changing the topic with a quick glance at her neck and face. Lilidh touched the sensitive areas and knew her skin showed every place that had been roughly touched by Symon or one of his men during the kidnapping. This time, she knew it wrong to let Rob take the blame.

'Much of it was during my capture,' she said. And she left it at that, not wanting to say more. 'I fought back,' she could not help but add.

Siusan nodded and then they both became busy

with chores. But the woman kept a watch on her, allowing no one to get too close and permitting short rest times throughout the day. By the time the evening meal had been made and served and the pots cleaned, exhaustion claimed her. And the thought of climbing those stairs terrified her.

Lilidh was sitting in the corner as the kitchen emptied, all the tasks of the day completed and the morrow's begun, when two guards entered and walked to where she waited. Siusan had left, as well, and if Lilidh had possessed the strength, she would have stood. She couldn't, so she watched their approach.

'Come with us,' one of them ordered. She looked from one to the other and knew they were only carrying out their duty in this.

Lilidh tried to push to her feet, but she stumbled and landed hard on the stool. Wincing, she tried again and failed. She was not trying to refuse—her body had simply given out. She did not resist when they took her by the arms, one on each side of her, and lifted her to her feet.

She lost track of herself then, as they hauled her along corridors and up the stairs to Rob's chambers. Truly, she would never have made her way without one at each arm. Lilidh leaned on their strength and let them carry her all the way and though they did not relent, they did not do this harshly. They reached the bedchamber and walked her in, releasing her next to the bed. The door had only just closed when she collapsed to the floor.

And she stayed as she fell.

Chapter Eight

The sight before his eyes shocked and horrified him.

He'd seen battles. He'd seen the dead. And he'd seen everything in between. But the sight of Lilidh, on his bedchamber floor, unmanned, undid him. Rob leaned down nearer to her and touched her face.

Thank the Almighty, she was still breathing.

She lay curled on her side, one arm tucked under her head and the other wrapped in her skirts. Though breathing, her chest barely moved. Her face, pale this morn, was ghostly now, washed of all colour. He spoke her name and received no response at all. Then, when he gently rubbed her shoulder, she moaned something he could not understand and rolled away from his touch. Glancing around the chamber, he found a basin and some water heated by the hearth and brought it closer to her.

When she'd entered the hall, so proud and fearless, his lungs had stopped taking in air. He watched her progress through the others, ignoring the insults and whispers that even he could hear until she stood before them. Everyone else disappeared as he took her in, truly for the first time.

The first thing he noticed was the pallor of her skin and the bruises that marred it. Her neck, chin, even her face, carried the evidence of harsh treatment—from Symon during her capture, no doubt. From the whiteness of her skin, he knew that there would be other marks on her arms and legs from his manhandling.

The first warning that more trouble was brewing for him came when Symon demanded to see Lilidh this morn. Tyra asked about her presence, which surprised him. Surely Symon had spoken to his sister about his plans and that Rob had claimed Lilidh. To speak plainly of her and to summon her publicly was out of character for his betrothed. As he'd told Symon, his choice of

women to take to his bed was his own business
and Tyra could neither question nor oppose it.

So, he supposed that surprise made him allow
the summons to bring Lilidh to happen. The demand that she work for her keep was another
surprise. It was as though Symon was calling his
bluff over her and over his disregard of the possible tender feelings of his sister.

A challenge, pure and simple, and one meant
to call his decision into question.

But Rob had thought to work around that by
agreeing—so that Lilidh was seen by all and that
his order to have her work would show she was
nothing more than a hostage of war and not to
receive any special treatment.

What the hell had he been thinking?

He dipped a cloth in the water and touched
it to her cheek, wiping away some remnant of
dirt gained from her working in the kitchens.
He reached for a cup on the table and brought it
to her lips. Lifting her head, he tipped it, allowing the ale to flow against her mouth until she
opened and took some. Her eyelids fluttered and
opened, her gaze confused and indistinct.

Then she realised where she was and who held

the cup. He got barely a second's warning before she pulled away from him and scooted across the floor. Not until she was pressed against the wall did she stop, her eyes now wild and her hands fending off anyone who approached. Rob followed with the cup, letting her come to full consciousness before speaking. When she took it from him and drank it down, he knew she was awake.

'Have you eaten?' he asked, taking the cup and filling it with half as much as before for her. Too much ale on an empty stomach would not be good for her.

Lilidh nodded, as she let her legs slide down in front of her. 'Siusan saw me fed.'

'Are you well?' he asked, rising to stand and holding out his hand to her. She waved it off.

'Well enough.'

He allowed her to remain there and tended to some letters that had arrived for him. Sitting at the table, he gave her time to gather herself before trying to speak more to her. Tossing the missives aside, he wondered if her father would send something in writing or in armour to answer this action of Symon's.

'Why did you do this? Why did you bring me into the middle of this?' she asked, unwilling to wait any longer for an explanation from him. 'What do you expect to get in return for me?'

Rob did not know how to answer her because he had yet to figure it out for himself. Some of it was obvious, but some was much more difficult to think about. His long-dead dreams kept raising themselves, poking and prodding his heart and his honour. For now, he would keep this situation between them as simple as possible. Without facing her, he gave her the easiest answer.

'Gold,' he said.

'Why do you lie to me over this? I deserve at least the truth of it from you.' How could she tell he lied?

'Leave it, Lilidh. You are here.' Rob faced her now and recognised the mutinous gleam in her eyes. She would not let this or much go untouched.

'Have you sent your demands to my father or the MacGregors yet?' she asked quietly, as though she could read his thoughts. 'Or heard from them yet?'

'Yes. Word of your presence here was sent

yesterday to both, though I suspect your father knows already.'

She shifted against the wall, drawing in a quick gasp as she moved. Her leg. She'd limped into the hall and out of it this morn. Now, after a day in the kitchens...

'Lilidh—' he began.

'Rob,' she interrupted. He paused and nodded to her to continue. His coming to his senses about her treatment and decision not to let his cousin, or his betrothed, give the orders could wait.

'Though I suspect the outcome might be no different, there is something you should know,' she said. The frown on her brow bespoke of news he would not like. 'I am not certain if your aim is war with both the MacLeries and the MacGregors or not.' She shifted again, pulling her legs up towards her chest and wrapping her arms around them. She was waiting for him to respond.

'Taking you prisoner involves both, I think. Neither your father nor your husband will suffer the insult to their honour lightly.'

'He is dead,' she said, almost on a whisper.

'Connor is dead?' he asked, going to her before he even knew he'd stood or taken a step.

'Your father…' Somehow he could never picture the ruthless, unbeatable Highland warrior dead. Regret rather than satisfaction pierced him. So many regrets.

'Not my father. Iain MacGregor. My husband died recently.' She shrugged. 'Though as his widow, I am sure his family will take insult since that's how you meant this to be.'

Dear God! Knowing the MacGregors, they would declare war against his clan just for the fun of fighting! This changed many things, especially since it made Connor the only one with whom they would be dealing. No one to argue or to mitigate with him on their behalf. Though Rob knew Connor paid heed to his wife and, now that Rob held Lilidh prisoner, Jocelyn would press for war against him. No mother was more dangerous when defending her young than the wife of the Beast.

Rob rubbed his face and turned away from Lilidh. Could this get any more tangled? Had Symon had any inkling of what they would face when he launched into this folly? And now, as chieftain, it was Rob's duty to get them out of it and save the clan, as well.

Then the truth of the matter struck him—Lilidh's husband was dead.

'When did he pass?' Rob asked as he faced her. He searched her expression for some sign of grief over the loss.

'Nigh to a month ago now,' she said in a calm voice. A tone far too calm for a wife missing her beloved husband, he thought.

If she was returning to Lairig Dubh when taken by Symon, then surely she could not be carrying an heir? Was she returning to tell her parents of the news?

'And his heir?' he asked, unexpectedly nervous over the answer. Somehow the thought of her carrying the child of Iain MacGregor turned his stomach. A political marriage, he had no doubt, but the image of her in that old man's bed forced Rob to confront many of his old feelings and desires and dreams.

'His brother has taken his seat as chief,' she explained without having to say more.

She carried no child of Iain MacGregor in her womb.

The implications ran furiously through his mind now. The problems. The possibilities. So much to consider and so much to make sense of before taking the next step. It was obvious that the MacGregors were concerned over the shift of loyalties in the area or the news of a new laird would have been announced. The MacKenzies could not have known of it or they would have shifted their attentions and attempts for new allies to the larger, more powerful, wealthier MacGregors over his clan. Would they now leave the Mathesons to face the rage of the MacLerie on their own?

He turned his attention back to the woman in the centre of all of this. He'd still not commented on the death of her husband and she did not look as most women who were recently bereaved appeared.

'My condolences on your loss, Lady MacGregor,' he said, offering his words to her official title. He'd met and known Iain through his time as foster son to Connor and he seemed a fair man. The only thing he could hold against him was… No, he could not think that. 'His death was unexpected?'

At her curt nod, Rob understood that Lilidh would not respond well to pity or too much soft sympathy, so he did not offer that. Since she knew that her marriage had made the two clans allies, Rob did not ask more about it or examine his own feelings when they tried to push their way to the front of his thoughts. Instead, he walked to where she sat and held out his hands again, this time not allowing her to refuse.

'Come. Sitting on the cold floor will only make things worse,' he said. 'Did Siusan stay with you all day?' He'd sent a message to the woman as soon as he'd ordered Lilidh to the kitchens. She was trustworthy and would not torment or abuse Lilidh. He lifted her to her feet and did not release her until she'd taken several steps. When they reached the chair nearest the hearth, she took hold of it and used it to keep her balance.

'Yes, she did. I do not remember her, but she said she'd visited Lairig Dubh years ago,' Lilidh said. Pushing her now-loosened hair out of her face and over her shoulders, she took in and released a deep breath. 'May I wash?' she asked, pointing at the basin where he'd left it on the floor.

Rob got the basin, added more hot water to it and placed it on the chair before her. After watching her for a few moments, he turned his back and gave her some privacy. It gave him time to sort out his thoughts.

If he did not take command of everyone in the clan, Lilidh would not be the only one in danger. He had been surprised, much as Symon had been, when he was named his father's successor, but if he did not step in and fully accept it, so much would be lost in lives and more. Looking back now at Lilidh, Rob knew he would not allow her to be mistreated while in his custody. He might allow others to think what they would, but no one else would give orders about her again.

This might be his first step—it would not be his last.

He would discover the truth about Symon's involvement with both the MacKenzies and, if any, his father's death. He would convince the elders who stood at Symon's side to come to his. And whether the MacKenzies or the MacLeries held the best opportunities for the Mathesons, he would discover it and make the best treaty for his clan.

Unfortunately, Symon was more entrenched and well established here than Rob was since he had expected and had been expected to inherit if

Ailean, his father's wife, did not give birth to a legitimate son. Only when his father began to question Symon's loyalty had the elders wavered in their unconditional support for his cousin. Then, when his father had changed his opinion and resisted the MacKenzies' overture to a better treaty with them and breaking with the MacLeries, had Rob's name been brought up as a possibility for tanist.

His father and Ailean's untimely deaths took away most of the choices or the time for the elders to evaluate who should be laird next. When their decision was needed, they chose Rob.

Though tradition called for the chieftain's chair to move through male heirs, their clan had also looked to female lines if needed and Symon's claim through his mother would stand. Yet, more than once legitimacy or the lack of it had been overlooked when the clan was in need. Since they were more landowners than nobles, the Mathesons were nothing if not practical when times called for it and these times did just that. But that did not mean that some would be unhappy or that some would try to change the decision of the elders.

Well, no matter, he was chief. And he had it in his power to remain in that position and to be an even better laird than his father had been. One very much like the man who now wanted his head separated from his shoulders and other bits of him torn apart, too.

'May I walk a bit?' Lilidh's voice broke into his reverie.

'Walk?' he asked, facing her. 'Where?'

'I just need to walk out some of the cramping,' she explained. 'Here would be fine.'

'And that doesn't hurt more than sitting or lying down?' He should have not asked about something so personal, something he had no right to question her about. Her expression exposed how much she hated to speak of her leg, but he wanted to know.

'Standing in one place. Sitting in one place. Too many steps. All of those hurt the most. Moving slowly, steadily, walking, even some riding is bearable,' she said.

'And today?'

She looked as though she had something to say and then just shook her head instead. Her hair, freed from the earlier braid, fell in waves over her shoulders and down her back, the midnight tresses made even curlier from the form and tightness of the plait. The dark circles under her eyes and the increasing pallor of her skin worried him.

'Go ahead,' he said, motioning with his hand across the length of the chamber. 'Have your walk.'

She gave him an uncertain glance and then bent down and removed her shoes. Lilidh remained leaning over, with her nose nearly touching her knees for several seconds. Then she straightened up and began taking longish strides across his chamber. He watched her for a bit, but decided he should focus his attentions on something other than the beautiful woman gliding along his bedchamber floor.

He picked up the papers that lay strewn across his table and put them in order. The MacKenzies had written, offering their terms for a new treaty, in language that sounded like a good deal. But the words seemed too flowery and too good to be the truth in deed. What he wouldn't give to have the MacLerie peacemaker look it over and give him advice.

The insanity of that thought made him realise how exhausted he was and how few options he and his clan had at this time. Either accept the MacKenzies and convince them to help fight off the MacLeries or, now forced into confrontation, be exterminated by the overwhelming fighting strength of the larger clan. Unfortunately, Symon had taken steps which forced him to do the first without completely preventing the second from happening.

The third time she passed by him, he put the letters down and watched her, openly. Her leg moved with more ease each time she paced the length of the chamber. She did not stumble now as she had at the beginning. Somehow she must have realised he was not reading and that he was now observing her closely. When she raised her eyes from the floor and her path and met his gaze, she tripped and began to fall.

He was out of his chair before his mind knew he was moving.

Chapter Nine

His strong arms encircled her, catching her before she landed on the floor. His motion still took them down, but he cushioned her body in his and suffered the brunt of the fall. Rob rolled them on the floor and they came to a stop in front of the hearth.

'Are you hurt?' he asked, helping her back up, but never quite taking his hands from her. And for one moment, God forgive her, she wished he would never let her go. Allowing herself that momentary lapse in reason, she gathered her hair that had tangled around them both in her hands and tugged it free.

'No,' she said, easing herself away from him. 'My thanks for catching me.'

'Mayhap you have walked enough for today?'

Rob poured ale in two cups this time and

handed one to her. Lilidh sat on the chair and sipped from the cup. Her thoughts were clear now, more so than they had been these last days and she wanted to know so much about what was going on and how this all had come to pass. Did she dare ask? She waited until he had approached the table covered in letters and documents before trying.

'So, you still have not told me what this is all about, Rob.' She sipped once more and dared a look at him. 'And why me? Why now?'

That needy, wistful part of her that wanted him to declare his undying love and that this was all just to get her back pushed its way to the surface of her feelings, leaving her more vulnerable than she'd felt in a long time. And considering that the man before her had cruelly disavowed her the last time they'd met, that revealed much to her. He took in and released a deep breath, but the tiny twitch of his left brow gave him away before the lie left his lips.

Much as it had all those years ago.

Before his words tore her world and heart apart.

'We are a poor clan and need the gold your father will pay for your safe return.'

'And from the MacGregors, as well, since you thought me still married to Iain?' she asked, probing for the truth. A flash of sympathy and pity crossed his gaze and then it was gone. For her? For her loss? She knew not.

'Both are prosperous, so, yes,' he answered, the twitch giving away his reply before he spoke. Did he even realise he did that? Gave himself away so clearly? Or had no one other than she recognised it? Most likely no one paid as much attention to his face and expressions as she had during their time together.

'Do you think my father will pay for my release?'

This was the pivotal question, for Lilidh understood exactly where she stood in her father's regard and what he must do against this insult. And paying for her return was not what he would do. Did Rob remember what he'd learned from the *Beast of the Highlands* from his fostering years in her family?

When silence was the only thing that hung in the space between them, she knew he did remember how her father responded to insults or threats. Lilidh drank down the rest of the ale and placed the cup back on the small table. The exhaustion of the day and the toll of the last several weighed down on her then. There was one more question she must ask.

'What is to become of me here, Rob?' She was going to add 'before my father arrives', but did not. He began to say something and stopped, then once more. Finally he spoke.

'You are under my protection now,' he replied.

'And what must I do to keep that protection?'

Once again, he paused and then tried to say several things at the same time. 'I have said it, so it continues until—'

'Do I work in the kitchens on the morrow?' she asked. She could never resist poking at him or her brother.

'I think that is best.' Ah, an answer. Her leg would not be able to manage those stairs day after day. If that was going to be her fate here, then she really must throw herself on his mercy.

'If I am to work there, is there a place on the lower floor where you can hold me prisoner? I cannot…' Her hand slipped down to touch her thigh where the most damage had been done.

'No. You sleep here.' She was startled at the intensity of his tone. So that would be the way of it. He did intend to bed her and was just waiting for a time to do so.

Perhaps now would be that time? She swallowed her fear and nodded. It was hard enough for her to bring up her maimed leg and ask for an accommodation due to it, but she would not raise the subject again with him.

Not certain if she should move or if he would, she waited for his orders. She did not plan to allow him to do this without a struggle, for more than her honour would be in shambles if he did. She knew him, had watched him grow into the man he was now, and in spite of the miserable way in which he had tossed her aside before, there was honour at his core. Taking her against her will would tear him apart. Regardless if it was for the good of his clan or to prove something to his cousin.

It would tear him apart.

She raised her chin and closed her eyes. If she had to fight him off to keep them both intact, she would. But Lilidh prayed it would not come to that.

'Go to bed!' he barked out in a brusque tone.

She jumped even though she tried not to. Rob filled another cup with ale and turned away from her. When his attentions were elsewhere, she limped over to the bed and climbed up on top of it.

'Lilidh,' he said softly. The devil come to call? She met his gaze and waited on him. 'Get undressed. Take your rest without worry this night.'

Another reprieve? Would he sleep in the same bed and not touch her? Her body ached. Her head ached. Every part of her screamed out in complaint, so she decided to take him at his word. She loosened the gown and pulled it over her head. The stockings remained in place mostly because her feet were chilled. The shift for obvious reasons. Tugging the thick bedcovers free, she climbed in under them and settled on one of the fluffy pillows. By the time her head touched that pillow, sleep was overtaking her.

A fine defence she would raise if Rob did indeed try anything. Would sleep ward him off one more time?

The birds of morning sung her from her sleep. Sunlight poured through the window high up on the wall of Rob's chamber.

Rob's chamber?

Rob?

Lilidh opened her eyes and found the bed empty save for her. Although an imprint dented the pillow next to the one where she'd slept, the bed's surface was cool to her touch. If Rob had slept next to her, he was long gone.

Pushing her hair away from her face, she slid up against the headboard of the bed and glanced around the chamber. From the amount of sun and the angle of the light, she guessed it must be nigh to mid-morn. And she was still in bed?

A tray holding a small pot and a wrapped bundle sat next to her on the table. Touching the pot, Lilidh found it yet warm, though not hot. Unwilling to leave the snug cocoon of bedcovers and also reluctant to allow the food and drink to go to waste, she decided to remain where she was until summoned once more into the fray. Or to the kitchens, whichever happened first.

The betony tea warmed and soothed her as it had before and the bread and cheese filled her belly. Soon, she grew restless sitting in the bed, so she slid out and stood while her leg became accustomed to standing. A clean, though plain, gown and a clean shift lay on the chair waiting for her. Dressing quickly, Lilidh found herself with nothing to do and nowhere to go.

Footsteps down the long corridor drew her attention. From the sound, she thought it might be Beathas. When the door opened, it was the old woman who entered, carrying a basket on her arm.

'You look better this morn, dearie,' she said with a smile. 'Let me have a look at your head.'

She pointed at the chair, so Lilidh sat and let her examine the lump that felt less swollen now than yesterday. And each touch felt less sharp than it had even the night before. A good sign, she hoped.

'Does your head still ache?' Beathas asked her.

'Not so much this morn.' A few moments later, the examination was done.

'How are the bruises?' The old woman's gaze softened as it fell on her neck and face.

Lilidh shrugged. As long as she did not press or explore them, she did not feel them. ''Tis well.'

A niggling feeling that Beathas thought Rob responsible for something more than he was bothered her again. The harsh treatment of Symon and his men caused the bruises—Beathas must know that because she saw to her needs from the first. But the woman's sympathy spoke of something else.

Desperate to divert Beathas's attention to the matter, she stammered out a question instead.

'Why was I not summoned to the kitchens this morn? It must be quickly approaching midday,' she said, accepting the brush from Beathas and beginning to tame the unruly curls on her head now that the dressing had been removed.

'The laird has given new orders,' she began. 'You are to remain here after all.'

'He has? I am?' Rob had seemed resolute last night, and now?

'Aye. You are to stay in this chamber and the corridor. He said you can walk the length of it if need be,' Beathas explained. The woman watched her closely as she explained Rob's new commands about her. Did she think him trying to assuage the guilt from other actions by being kinder now?

'Did anyone argue with him when he ordered this change?' she asked. Surely Symon and his sister would.

'Did not listen to them,' she said with a chuckle. 'He brushed their words aside and said there were too many ways for you to escape through the kitchens. Safer to keep you in here, where no one could get to you and you could no' get far.'

With her leg as it was, she could not get down the steps to escape. Hmmm. She had not thought about escape possibilities from the kitchen when she'd been there. She needed to use her mind and keep an eye open for such opportunities. It would take some time for her father to plan his attack and she needed to use that to discover whatever she could about the Mathesons' strengths and weaknesses. She knew he would try to negotiate first because she was being held.

So, she would also try to encourage Rob to look for a peaceful way out of this situation for all of them before the MacLeries arrived in force.

Beathas finished just as Siusan arrived carrying a large basket of clothing and another smaller basket filled with threads and sewing supplies. Lilidh stood to greet her.

'Your work for the day,' Siusan announced, putting it near the chair on the floor and handing her the smaller basket. If the woman was pleased not to have Lilidh under foot in the kitchens, Lilidh could not tell. Her tone gave no hint of her feelings on the matter.

'What is this?' she asked, reaching into the basket and pulling out a tunic.

'His lairdship's laundry, of course. For you to repair.' Lilidh dropped it back in the basket and looked at Siusan. 'He has no wife and there is no lady in charge of such things yet.'

'Tyra does not oversee this for Rob?'

'Their betrothal is only a recent thing. Mayhap once this is all settled.'

Betrothal? Rob was betrothed to that woman and never said anything to her? No small wonder that the lady reacted as she had to Lilidh's presence in the hall. Especially if she believed Rob and Lilidh were lovers. Wives usually had to learn forbearance when it came to other women their husbands chose and, in the case of lairds and chiefs and nobles, those other women could be quite public.

Still, betrothed to that woman? A topic to discuss with the man who now claimed her as his and not for this servant's ears.

'From the kitchens to this,' she said, bringing

their conversation back to the task before her. 'Is he not afraid I'll sew all the seams shut? Can I be trusted with scissors?'

'Lady Tyra raised those very questions to the laird.'

She could see the mirth in the older woman's blue eyes. Oh, to have been a witness to this scene! It would have almost made things funny. Almost. 'And?'

'She will not be raising those questions again,' she explained. 'The laird made it clear what her position in his hall is and what is his.'

Stunned that he had taken a public stance against Symon and Tyra on this, Lilidh sat down on the chair and lifted the tunic once more. Searching in the smaller basket, she found a matching thread and began to sew the tear along the seam closed. Embroidering and sewing were always a great way to clear her thoughts and her mother had always encouraged her skill in it.

'I will come back later with more,' Siusan said as she walked to the door. Beathas left at the same time and she listened as they walked away, chatting quietly as they went.

Well, if nothing else, she would be busy. There

must be at least six or seven tunics and trews as well as shirts. It would take her most of the day to finish these, but she did not have to walk down those steps and that was a good thing.

More importantly, Rob *had* heard her words and fears about her leg and done something about it. For her. What had happened to make him take her side, especially against his betrothed? Since she did not want to give anyone there a reason to return her to the kitchens, Lilidh decided to work on mending the clothes. When her leg began to cramp from sitting too long in one position, she stood and paced the chamber.

Did he mean for her to be allowed out of the chamber?

Should she try?

Making her way over to the door, she lifted the latch and peered out. The two guards on duty immediately blocked the door, preventing her from leaving at all.

'Beathas said I may walk,' she said, glancing from one to the other. She fully expected them to order her back inside, so when they parted and nodded permission to her, she paused before stepping into the corridor.

Lilidh worried through the first few paces, but then each one became a bit easier. Each guard walked to the opposite end of the corridor and blocked it so that none could leave or enter from the stairs. Though several times they looked as though they wanted to say something to her, they never did. Not wanting to bring any untoward attentions by remaining there too long, she covered the length of it four times, counting the paces between one end and the other.

Counting the paces between the three chambers on one side and two on the other. Counting how many paces it took to reach the stairway. By the time her leg was loose and somewhat comfortable, she had memorised the locations and distances to all the rooms on this floor.

Her father would be proud.

When she returned to the bedchamber, Lilidh took some of the thicker threads and tied knots to remember all the calculations she'd made. Then she tucked the threads into her sleeve to keep it safe for when she needed it. For that moment, it felt good to be thinking ahead. To be making a plan.

* * *

The next interruption to her work came when a tray was delivered to her as sunset approached. Standing and stretching as a servant she'd seen in the kitchens entered with it, Lilidh waited while the girl put it on the bigger table on the other side of the room. Since Rob had left parchments scattered over its surface, she gathered them into a pile and moved them so as not to damage them.

Once alone, the documents proved too much temptation for her and she reached for the one on top of the pile and read it.

Latin was no obstacle for her—she could read in several languages, though not as easily as her cousin Ciara could. Ciara was permitted to work with her father on contracts and such while Lilidh had only been allowed to watch silently during some sessions.

Watch and learn, lass, her father and uncle instructed.

So she did, and she had learned much about the workings between clans and about contracts and, more importantly, about men. How they thought. The reasons behind their decisions. Now, looking over this offer of *friendship* from the MacKenzies, Lilidh understood the difficult place Rob was in.

The old laird had been approached and given some indication of willingness to switch his allegiance from the MacLeries to the MacKenzies—a move that had far-reaching implications. An alliance between them would shift the balance of power in the west of Scotland and create instability where her father strived for peace. On his terms, certainly, but peace and stability.

Still, there was nothing except a long-standing relationship to keep the ties strong between the Mathesons and the MacLeries. The old laird's regard and friendship had resulted in Angus sending his illegitimate son to foster with her family. And that her father accepted Rob spoke of the respect between the two men. Until he had repudiated their love and humiliated her before all.

And now? How would Rob go? If he had ordered her kidnapping, clearly he was trying to tweak her father's nose as he left. Worse, he was trying to bring her family into war, for if the MacLeries rose against the Mathesons, the MacKenzies' offer of support in this letter alone would guarantee their involvement. Had she become the instrument of war to bring down her powerful family and redistribute the power and wealth in the western Highlands?

Perhaps the other letters and documents held the answer to that critical question. It was as she reached for another missive that she heard the footsteps approaching the door. The heavier step and pace told her it was a man. When she heard the voices outside the door, she knew Rob had returned to his chambers.

Lifting the tray and carrying it to the bed, she then scattered the documents across the table, hoping Rob would not notice. Going back to the bed, she slid onto it and brought the tray nearer to make it appear as though she'd eaten there and not gone near to the table. When the door opened, she stuffed a piece of bread in her mouth and tried not to look guilty.

Chapter Ten

When he'd awoken at dawn's light, Rob had discovered her tucked against him, but even then, hardly moved from the night before. A man's presence in her bed did not disturb her rest, even if she did not remember which man it was at her side. Cursing himself for that thought and the resentment it caused within him, Rob carefully peeled himself away from her and climbed from the bed. Certainly she was accustomed to a man at her side—she'd been married for months. At least until Iain died, whenever that was. Glancing back at her, he noticed that Lilidh did not move.

Siusan told him she worked without complaint and with little pause through the day. She'd mentioned that Lilidh had some difficulty sitting and gave him a glaring look, but he dismissed it and her without understanding it. The expression was matched throughout the day by others, all from women, and all without further comment. Puzzling, but he had little time to think about that when so many other more important matters lay in his lap.

He had dressed quickly and left the chamber, giving the guards new instructions. Although he'd not said so, he knew Lilidh's leg was the reason for her request to be held nearer to the kitchens. But his reaction to her request told him much about himself and his continuing attraction to this woman.

The day passed quickly for him, but if he tried to convince himself that he gave her no thought, Dougal's smirk told him otherwise. The man was too observant, though he never said a word.

They rode to the boundaries of their land to check for any sign of intruders. He knew the MacLeries would arrive any day now and wanted as much warning as possible. Rob set more guards along the road to give him that warning. More of the villagers and farmers arrived each day, called in to the keep for safety. Their lands and most livestock would still be in danger, but there was little he could do about that.

Though he complained all day long, Symon accompanied them, along with several others loyal to Rob. Better to keep him close at hand during these times than discover he'd caused more problems. Symon's defensive strategies, when Rob finally got him to speak, were good ones, especially for their smaller numbers facing a larger force. His cousin's surprise when Rob ordered them implemented made him laugh.

Genuine surprise filled Symon's gaze when Rob shared the news of Iain MacGregor's recent death. Was the kidnapping an unplanned event after all? But there'd been no explanation about how Symon knew Lilidh was travelling back to Lairig Dubh.

When he thought about it, he really did not want to find out that Symon was involved with his father's death. They'd abided each other as children and young men and Symon had qualities that would make him an effective counsellor— if he could get past his anger and accept Rob as laird and chief. With Dougal overseeing the keep and lands and Symon as the commander of his warriors, Rob could see the Mathesons as a clan to be reckoned with.

They had many hurdles and obstacles to clear before any of that could happen. Indeed, there was every possibility that he and Dougal and Symon would be dead when all this played out and his clan torn apart and spread across the Highlands.

Connor had taught him that behind anger was usually fear and that was something few men could admit to having. Was this the basis for Symon's anger—fear that he would have no place or be forsaken and unnecessary if Rob was chief? Or that his sister would be cast aside?

Rob had been so eager not to appear the fool, he might have ignored Symon's suggestions or advice, believing that he must be in charge and come up with the best plans. Now, removed from most of his cronies, Symon spoke more openly and less aggressively than with them. Rob decided to involve his cousin in planning how to deal with the MacLeries.

By the time they returned to the keep, there was a tentative peace between them and Rob hoped he was wrong about Symon's connection to what had happened to his father and Ailean.

Any rapport between them evaporated as they took dinner in the hall. Any steps to reconciling were lost as Symon's men and supporters pulled Symon back into the anger. Tyra, whose demeanour had changed as soon as Lilidh arrived, reacted to every mention of her name even though Rob refused to discuss Lilidh with anyone.

Not that he did not understand how his actions—claiming Lilidh as his before the entire hall—caused her ill temperedness. He did. And if his or her feelings were one bit engaged, he would care. But their betrothal would be one of convenience and for political reasons and not based on personal regard for each other. He knew it. She knew it. And, for now, he could not allow anyone to contradict or overrule him this matter regardless of any arrangements made for the future.

Dinner had become a battleground once more with brother and sister picking at each other and him with pointed barbs and implied insults. Finally, exercising his power once more, he had ended it by sending Tyra to her chambers before the last food was served.

Symon had remained only because he had arrangements to discuss with him. After a promising beginning to the day, it had gone to hell faster than he believed possible, leaving him with the nearly irresistible urge to throw both of his cousins from the battlements with millstones, very large millstones, tied around their necks! He would think about the matter of Symon and how to find out his truths later.

Now, as he approached his chambers, he wondered how Lilidh would be. Was she pleased at the reprieve from the kitchen, or rather the steps, that he ordered this morn? Were his garments in worse shape than before?

But the biggest question was whether or not she would admit to reading the documents he'd left and would she speak about them?

'Did she eat?' he asked Tomas.

'Aye, just now.'

'Did she walk?'

'Some. Earlier in the day,' Tomas replied. 'She's been quiet since Beathas and Siusan left her.'

'No questions from her? No requests?' Her

sense of curiosity had amazed him when they were young. 'Why?' or 'how?' were her most commonly spoken words. If she was feeling better, if her injuries were healing, she would begin asking soon. He hoped she had not lost that trait as she'd grown up and left Lairig Dubh.

When they shook their heads at him, he dismissed them and lifted the latch on his door. Lilidh slid off the bed and stood, chewing something from the tray of food as she did.

'You look well. How is your head?' he asked as he dropped his leather sack by the bed and glanced around the room.

'Better,' she said after she swallowed.

She looked better—some colour back in her cheeks, not limping or wincing as much as last night. The fire was low and the room growing cool, so he put fresh wood in the hearth and got it back aflame.

'Rob,' she said softly and his body burned hotter than the hearth did at the sound of it. He stood quickly and turned to find her staring at him.

'Yes?' he forced out.

All she needed to do was utter his name in that voice and he lost his mind and almost let loose his self-control. She had haunted his dreams for so long before he finally banished the memories of their times together. And yet, every moment with her, brought them back in ways he could hear and taste and feel.

'I am grateful to you for allowing me to stay here this day,' she began, twisting her fingers in the fabric of her gown. 'I know you changed your orders about me in front of your people and how difficult that may make things for you.'

'It is safer this way,' he answered, trying to keep his tone light and resist the urge to take her in his arms and kiss the very breath from her. 'You might escape through the kitchens.'

He watched the corners of her mouth lift and held his breath as her green eyes brightened, releasing the tension in her face and making her look as she did when she was ten-and-six years to his ten-and-eight. They would steal minutes or hours when they could, exploring new feelings and boundaries, until in one, brief, catastrophic moment he had ruined everything and lost her for ever.

'I finished fixing your clothes,' she said, pointing to a large basket of folded garments by the chair. 'Since apparently your betrothed does not see to such things for you.'

Damn! Unable yet to think of Tyra as his betrothed, he'd also failed to mention it to Lilidh. Word travelled quickly, though, and now…

'The elders requested the match, Lilidh. Surely you of all people can understand a political marriage.'

Her green eyes flashed and then went blank. She understood. Believing there was nothing else to say on the matter and unable to wait, he asked the question he most wanted to know.

'How long did you hesitate before reading them?'

A myriad of emotions and reactions passed quickly across her lovely face as she decided what to say. Her expression went to one of innocence. He'd known her too well and for too long to believe her attempt to avoid answering.

'Did you wait until after you'd walked?'

She spun away from him, placing herself between him and the table. Reaching over, she selected one of the documents and held it out to him. 'I was so busy with my chores that I only just noticed this.'

Rob took the letter and read it quickly, identifying exactly what she'd read—the MacKenzies' final offer of 'friendship' to his father before his death. Some of it puzzled him. Some of the reasons to switch allegiances made no sense as though only half the conversation was being heard. What he wanted most right now, after the woman herself, was her reaction to the offer.

'And?' he prodded.

She stared at him for a second or two before laughing. The glorious sound of that laughter, in the midst of such a time and place and situation, gladdened his soul that she was here. Regardless of the strange and dangerous circumstances of her being in Keppoch, he was glad of it.

'You did it on purpose, did you not?' she asked as she continued to watch him intently. 'You left them all over the table because you wanted me to see these.' Lilidh crossed her arms over her chest and stared once more.

'Maybe I had no objections to your seeing them?' He mimicked her stance and raised his brow.

She released a breath and looked at the documents on the table. Shrugging, she pointed at the one he yet held.

'This was addressed to your father? Before his death?' He nodded. 'And it is the first exchange? The first contact?'

'Something is missing, is it not?' He asked her the question that had bothered him the most.

Before she could give her answer, the sound of feet shuffling by stopped her. Rob looked towards the door, expecting it to open. When it did not, he strode to it and lifted the latch. No one was there.

He'd dismissed the guards, so it was no surprise that they'd left. Glancing down the corridor in both directions, towards the stairs and the other end, he saw and heard no one. None of the doors to the other chambers seemed disturbed, but he knew they'd heard someone outside his chambers. Turning to her, he put his finger over his lips. She nodded understanding. He closed the door and walked to her.

'Would you be able to manage one flight of steps without difficulty or pain?' he asked, looking for a cloak or something to protect her from the night's chill.

'Yes,' she said as puzzlement filled her gaze.

'Come then,' he directed her as he grabbed a thick blanket and tucked it under his arm.

Rob guided her out of his chambers and to the left, away from the stairs. At the end of the corridor, he turned right into a small alcove in front of a door. Lifting the latch and pushing the door open, he held it for Lilidh to enter.

This stairway was one of two that led to the battlements and the ruined tower above. Though guards were always on duty there, they were less likely to be overheard as he was sure had happened in his chambers. He took the steps slowly, allowing Lilidh to set the pace and supporting her as she climbed. Soon, they reached the doorway at the top and he opened it.

The wild winds pushed and pulled the door, so he held it firmly until she climbed the last step and walked through. Then the winds took her, buffeting her and tossing her hair around her like an impenetrable cloud. She laughed as she gathered it all in her hands and tied it with some leather strips she pulled from around her wrist. The thick tresses under control, she accepted the blanket he'd brought and pulled it around her shoulders.

'Walk a bit, but stay away from the edge,' he said. Then, as she began to take a few strides in the direction he'd indicated, he went to give the guards new orders. Lilidh had slowed her pace when he reached her and they walked silently to the other side of the keep's battlements from where they'd entered.

The sun's warmth was long gone and the moon had begun its rise in the east. There was enough light provided by that and the torches around the perimeter to see their path. Once they'd reached the place he had in mind, just next to the entrance to the ruined tower, he stopped.

'Who would spy on you in your chambers, Rob?' she asked before he could.

He'd been thinking the same thing. The guards said no one had entered from that door and they'd seen no one until Rob. No servants were expected on that floor until morning. His business with anyone in the clan was complete, so unless it was a gravely important matter, no one would seek him in his chambers. That only left nefarious reasons behind the presence and disappearance of an unknown soul.

'I can think of no one, save Symon,' he replied. Though after today, he wondered about his cousin. 'But I do not think it was him.'

At her puzzled expression, he explained more about his discussions with Symon this day and the change or difference Rob noticed in him when he took his cousin's opinion into consideration.

'What was it about that letter that gave you pause? You had suspicions before I mentioned mine.' She nodded and gathered the blanket tighter around her shoulders. Leaning her head lower to keep the wind from carrying her voice, she gave him the answer he was hoping for.

'It felt as though I was stepping in when a conversation was already going on between them. This letter referred to subjects and questions that clearly had been opened before this one was written. Is there an earlier one?'

That was it! She'd discovered the problem immediately. As he'd known her quick mind would.

'None that I could find in my father's papers.'

'Who was his clerk? Does he still serve you?

That would be a good place to begin,' she suggested.

'Brother Donal returned to the abbey when my father passed. I have a new clerk—Brother Finlay has taken over his duties now.'

And Brother Finlay had been recommended by Symon, having previously served Symon's father.

'From the look in your eyes, you have just realised something bad,' she said, gazing at him.

He shrugged, not ready to share this with her right now. She took a step away and then turned back to face him.

'So, if you will not answer that question, answer this one: why did you want me to see the documents?'

Should he be honest with her? Should he reveal the depth of the problems facing him to the daughter of his enemy? Well, that was not completely true, if he was being honest with himself. Connor might be the enemy of other clans and to some of his clansmen, but through it all, Rob had never considered them to be so. He smiled and met her astute gaze.

'I still find myself thinking about what he would do or how he would handle something

when faced with a task or a duty,' he admitted.
'He is the most intelligent and wise man I have
ever met or known. I usually begin considering
something with the words "what would Connor
think about this matter?"'

'And ruthless and cunning,' she added.

'Aye, that too.' He laughed as the man's daughter described in the words he'd avoided using. For
many reasons.

'And sometimes wrong, though he loathes to
admit such a thing is possible.' Lilidh laughed
softly, then grew more serious. 'So why has this
breach opened between you two and forced you
to be enemies? Why can you not go to him and
solve this without bloodshed or bravado?'

He shook his head and crossed his arms. 'That
is not possible.' For so many reasons he could
never admit to her. For so many reasons.

'So instead you kidnap his daughter and ask
her the questions you would ask him? You seek
out his advice from one who learned at his knee
along with you?'

From her tone, he could not tell if she was
pleased or angry. Her face gave no clue. 'Just
so, it would seem.'

'I cannot and will not speak for my father, Rob. You know that. But my advice would be to seek out someone you trust who knew your father when these letters were being exchanged and ask about it. There is more behind this offer and move on the MacKenzies' part than is being done in the open. Find out what. And...' she paused and looked at him '...you must break from the past and be your own man, Rob. You cannot be the laird that my father is or that your father was. You must claim the chair as your own in your own way.'

Exactly what the man under discussion would have counselled if he'd asked.

If it were only that easy. To break free from the past with all its promises, hopes and failures. To let go of the guilt he lived with every day and accept his place—his rightful place.

'Sound advice, as I expected, Lilidh,' he said.

It was not through any fault of hers that only one of the things she suggested could be done. The second, well, there was too much of the past still controlling him to accept it could be done easily or now. He held out his arm to her to take her back inside and she accepted it. They'd almost reached the stairway down to his chamber's floor when she pulled them to a stop.

'You at least owe me the truth, Rob. What lies between you and my father now? What keeps you from the friendship you once had?'

Try as he might, the word, the answer, pushed its way out before he could stop it.

'You.'

Chapter Eleven

For the first time since she'd been brought here, Lilidh faced going to bed somewhat awake. Or rather, his bed. The other nights had found her either in a stupor due to Beathas's concoction or without a bit of strength left in her from her day in the kitchen. This night—which began with several interesting revelations from Rob—now quieted into darkness and silence.

Rob returned to the chamber without saying another word and returned to studying the documents there. He'd left for some time with them and brought them back, but they exchanged no more words over them or anything else either. She wanted to speak on the matter more, for his admission had shocked her. In one word, he'd explained much and created even more questions for her.

As a child of the MacLerie laird, the Earl of Douran, who owned huge amounts of land and commanded one of the largest fighting forces in the Highlands, Lilidh knew his reputation and his true skills and temperament. And she knew her place in his world, exactly how she fit into his scheme of things and plans. She also knew that her father would never start a war for her.

Yet, in a way, that's exactly what Rob had said he had done over her.

In laying the blame at her feet, Rob forced her to think about the true relationship she had with her father and his past actions regarding her. Though she'd always thought of herself as a chattel in his world, valued and respected, but a chattel none the less, Rob's claim gave her pause now. And hope.

Not that she wanted war—she did not want that. But the fact that her father considered her feelings and the treatment she'd received at Rob's hands to be important enough to not only part ways but to break up their alliance—what did that mean now? Would he fight to get her back? Pitch his clan and their allies against Rob to bring her home?

She rolled to her side, moving off her bad leg, and tucked her hand under her head. Would sleep never come? She let out a sigh and closed her eyes. At least if she could seek her rest before he got into the bed, there might be a chance of avoiding the discomfiture of such a situation. When he began to move around the chamber, putting out candles and lanterns and then banking the flames in the hearth, she knew no way to avoid the coming situation.

Feigning sleep would be her only way. She forced her breaths to come at a slow and deep pace. Letting her body fall limp, she concentrated on not thinking about Rob, the first and only man who had touched her intimately, as he undressed and climbed into bed with her. Though he let several layers of bedcovers remain between them, her body reacted as if their naked flesh touched.

Trying again not to think about those matters, she counted the seconds of each inhalation and exhalation. Would concentrating on that distract her from the memories? But, then, as these things do, trying not to think about them simply brought them back more quickly and stronger than she could avoid.

Their last time together.

She'd sought him out in the cave they discovered in the forest outside Lairig Dubh. They met there often, sharing moments of privacy and daring all sorts of scandalous intimacies for which her father would have beaten her if he'd known. But they were in love, going to marry, so Lilidh allowed him some measure of liberty in touching and caressing her. His kisses were wicked things and she never would have imagined that a touching of the lips could be so exciting.

This day Rob dared more than before, making her body ache for every touch. Tension had built to unimaginable levels inside her and she knew Rob caused it—and could relieve it somehow if he would. As her body blossomed under his hand, he unlaced her gown, moved her shift down and touched his mouth there, kissing a sensuous path towards her breasts.

He slid his hand inside and teased the tautened tip of her breast with his thumb before taking it into his mouth! Her body shook at each caress and when his teeth tightened down on the sensitive tip, she screamed out, in surprise and excitement.

His laugh as he did these things was as wicked as what he did to her. Making her a creature she did not recognise. Making her want to allow him to do even more… To take the final step and join their bodies now.

'Hush, now,' he whispered. Though his words seemed aimed to calm things between them, his hand never stopped touching her breasts. 'We do not want to alert anyone that we are here, my love.'

Lilidh shook her head and could not gather any words together in that moment, for all she could do was feel the terrifying yet exhilarating way her heart raced and her skin heated. When his hand moved down over her gown and began to slide up her leg, she stopped breathing altogether.

She had not realised her eyes were closed until she'd opened them and found him staring at her. Lilidh lifted her hand and touched his face. His eyes burned with desire for her and she waited for seemingly unending moments until she felt his fingers touch the top of her thighs. He swirled them in circles, gently teasing her until her legs fell open.

Gasping as he moved ever deeper into that private place, she grabbed for his wrist to stop him. This could not be right. Could it?

'Sweet Lilidh,' he whispered. 'Do you wish me to stop now? Or can I show you the pleasure that can be between a man and the woman he loves?'

The devil lived on earth and his name was Rob Matheson.

Though she understood about how a man and woman joined—no one could live in a place such as Lairig Dubh and not understand it—no one had ever told her that this...this pleasurable touching was part of it. Or mayhap this was the part parents warned young women about when discussing the protection of their virtue? One touch and every warning ever heard melted away as the need for more burned through her body and soul.

'More,' she begged and he did. More. And kept doing more, proving his hand as wicked as his mouth, until that tension built so strong and so tight in her core that it had to break.

Her body arched and tightened and he relentlessly caressed her, until every bit of that splendid tension spilled out, leaving her empty and yet full at the same time.

And even now, four years later, her body still remembered his touch and wanted more.

If she continued to move and to breathe like that, he was going to lose control and take her once and for all.

Rob listened in the dark and Lilidh's breathing grew tight and tense. If she was dreaming, did she picture her husband pleasuring her? If awake, did she remember Iain's caresses now? Even a fool or madman would recognise the way she breathed, the way her body responded to being touched and caressed and...more.

Even his body reacted to hers—he hardened and begged for attention. Her attention. Her body. To finish the pleasure they'd begun all those years ago when she was to be his. A moan, one barely loud enough to be heard, whispered across the bed between them.

'More,' she whispered in a low, husky voice.

Rob bit his tongue to keep from saying anything. She must be dreaming. She must be. Even knowing that Iain must be at the centre of her thoughts did not lessen his burning desire for her.

His hands itched to reach over and touch her as he used to, when they loved. When he loved her.

How had her body changed since he'd touched her? How would it feel to move between her legs and fill the place that would make her his completely? They'd both had other lovers since last they met and now the act of joining would hold no fear and only pleasure for them. To see how the promise of passion in her had matured was something he'd thought about since their parting. Especially when the memories of their time together and how she had responded to his touch and his mouth haunted him in the nights alone.

Lilidh would be magnificent in the throes of pleasure. She shifted once more now, her hips lifting and lowering, and he almost begged her then. Just as his hand reached out to touch her face, she turned towards him and opened her eyes.

Glazed over with desire and pleasure, she searched his face as though she did not know him. Then, her gaze cleared and he could tell the moment when the circumstances and his identity returned to her. She moved away from him so quickly, he could not reach for her in time.

Her body slid over the side of his bed and hit the floor with a thud. The groan told him she'd landed on her injured leg. He moved across the bed and got out quickly, trying to help her to her feet, but she resisted, pulling back and tugging free of him from her place on the floor. Finally, he released her hand, knowing she must be embarrassed now that she understood he'd witnessed her dream.

Witnessed it? Hell, his body wanted to be part of whatever dream she was having. His arousal could not be mistaken if she'd seen it. Her wide eyes and opened mouth as she climbed to her feet said she had.

'Here, now,' he said, leaning over to help her stand. 'Did you hurt yourself?' Once she stood, he moved away, seeking the jug of ale on the table. They could both use something to drink, so he filled two cups and held one out to her. She shook her head, pulled a blanket free from the bed and sat in the chair near the now-cold hearth.

'I will be fine,' she said, her voice quivering as though she was ready to cry. Oh, God, no tears, please!

Had she grieved for her husband? Did these

dreams remind her of happier times in their marriage? They could not have been wed more than two or three months if Iain passed about a month ago. How much could she have loved him by then?

Rob remembered the day he received word of her betrothal to Iain MacGregor. He got drunk, very drunk, and came up with plans for how to stop the marriage. And they were good plans, too. Luckily, he sobered up the next day and knew it meant that he and Lilidh would never be together.

Well, he needed this ale now and he finished the full cup before stopping or facing her. When he turned back, she sat staring sightlessly into the empty hearth.

Deciding to give her the time she needed to deal with the memories that assaulted her now, Rob went back to bed. Minutes turned into hours and still she sat in the chair not speaking, not seeing, not sleeping either. When, about three hours later, her head began to nod and then dropped, he climbed from the bed and carried her to it.

His mind wandered the rest of the night as she slept quietly now in his bed. The advice she'd given him about what to do next swirled around in his thoughts with memories of her crying out in satisfaction the last time they were together. The way that she had begged him for more when he'd stopped touching her.

The way she had begged for more.

His body reacted before he realised that she was not remembering Iain in her dreams—she was remembering him.

He would find her another place to sleep in the morning.

Chapter Twelve

Lilidh woke with a start and discovered herself in Rob's bed again. Looking around the chamber, she found him gone, along with the documents and the large trunk that held more of them. She fell back on the pillow and tried not to think of how she'd humiliated herself last night.

The blood of a harlot must run in her veins from some long-ago, long-forgotten ancestor. At least that would explain the shameful display that had happened to her in Rob's bed, with him listening and watching. His nearness, her injuries and isolation and whatever else excuse she could draw on would be her defence. But it was her heart that was the real reason for her lapse in behaviour and her loss of control.

She had been so caught up in the memories that she never realised he was watching or that she'd said something aloud until she opened her eyes and saw him staring at her. Even now her cheeks burned as she remembered the look in his eyes at that moment.

It was the same one that she had seen there all those years ago when he had introduced her to the intensity that could be between them.

The night before he renounced her before her family because of the imperfection of her maimed leg. The night when she had thought her dreams of marrying the man she loved would come true. The night before she lost her innocence when she wanted to lose her virtue.

Well, this self-pity and embarrassment would get her nowhere this morn, so she pushed the covers back and dressed. She expected Beathas and Siusan would be arriving shortly. So, when the door opened, she turned from straightening the bed to greet one or the other.

Rob stood in the sin-revealing light of day and watched as she smoothed the bedcovers in place.

Words fled as she tried to think of what to say to him this morn, when the memories of their passion and his betrayal and her body's scandalous reactions were all very fresh in her mind. So she waited for him to speak instead.

'We are moving to another chamber,' he said, as he walked to one of his trunks and opened it. Searching inside for something and not finding it, he moved to the next one and repeated his actions. 'The last chamber on the left,' he said, now searching through several leather sacks.

He stared in her direction and when she nodded her understanding of his directions, he continued. 'You cannot walk in the corridor any longer. Many from the outlying villages are moving into the keep for protection and the elders will be using these rooms.'

'You have heard back from my father, then?' she finally asked.

'The messenger said he received my demands and is sending his reply,' Rob said.

A shiver made her body tremble. They both knew what that meant—and it wasn't that gold was on the way. Lilidh knew that gave them at least week, but not much more than that.

'What should I do?' she asked, waving her hand towards the trunks and furnishings in his chamber.

'Stay out of the way until you're told to move down the corridor.'

And with that one command, he was gone.

It did not take long for the servants, and guards, to arrive to move Rob's belongings. She remained in the chair, watching them, until the guard named Tomas ordered her to come along. Lilidh was almost to the last chamber near the stairs to the battlements when the door to the room next to it opened and Lady Tyra stepped out.

Tyra examined her from head to toe and her expression turned to one of disgust, as though she'd stepped her precious new slipper into something the horses dropped behind them. Part of her could understand the lady's anger now that she understood Tyra's relationship to Rob, but she should know that Lilidh had little or no control over her stay here.

'Is this your chamber, Lady Tyra?' Lilidh asked. The lady's gasp drew the attention of everyone in the now-busy corridor.

'Do not speak to me, you harlot!' she replied. The slap—though with her hand closed in a fist, it felt more like a punch—that accompanied the insult was the surprise. 'You may warm his bed and see to his baser needs, but do not think yourself worthy to speak to me.'

Lilidh recoiled from the blow and touched her cheek. She felt Tomas at her back, but pushed away from him. Truth be told, Lilidh had a higher standing as the daughter of an earl and laird than Tyra did. She should be glad that Lilidh *deigned* to speak to her!

'Guard! Get her out of my sight!' Tyra called out. Tomas moved forwards, taking Lilidh by the arm and leading her away.

'And worry not, whore,' Tyra whispered so only Lilidh could hear. 'Your days in his bed are numbered.'

The venom in her voice sent shards of ice and fire and terror through Lilidh. When Lilidh turned back to look at her face as Tomas dragged her the few paces to Rob's new chambers, Tyra's expression was blank. If one was just looking at her now, it would be impossible to believe the ugly words and tone she'd just spoken in to Lilidh. Tomas pushed her inside and closed the door, leaving her alone. Had she imagined the hatred and danger in the woman's words? Somehow she thought not.

Looking around her new quarters, she found a chamber twice the size of Rob's previous one. More of a surprise was the small cot in one corner, not far from the huge rope-strung bed that dominated the entire room. This one was much more like the one her parents shared— large enough for two and his business as laird, yet made more comfortable by small personal touches.

Rob's father's?

Seeing a basin and a bucket of water, she dipped a cloth in the water and placed it on her face, allowing the coolness to soothe the place where Tyra had struck her. Then she stayed out of the way while the servants completed the move of Rob's belongings here. And hers, it seemed, since one of her trunks also appeared with the others. When had that been retrieved?

Unable and unwilling to sit idly by while the servants worked to organise the chambers according to Rob's preferences, she found the basket of garments to be repaired, gathered some threads and a needle and sat working. She did not miss the gossip that the women especially began whispering as they worked. Lilidh kept her head down as though she did not hear them, letting them sink back into the invisibility in which servants usually existed.

Lilidh discovered several interesting things from the servants over the hour or so that they worked there.

This had, indeed, been Rob's father's chamber when he was alive and Rob had refused to use it until now.

Rob's cousin Symon had kidnapped her without Rob's consent.

The last thing was the worst—they all expected to be dead once her father arrived.

Having the reputation that her father had and having earned most of it was a distinct advantage in war. Lilidh understood that. But to hear these people speak of their deaths so openly was horrible. Her father did not simply put innocents to death—his enemy in this would suffer, not them. For now, she chose not to correct their misassumptions, for they were a distinct advantage for her father and hopefully would bring this all to a peaceful close.

And then she would be returned to her parents to be given away again, leaving the only man she had ever loved behind once more. In spite of the horror at his earlier actions and the desperate anger and dejection at his disavowal, she could not deny that she had loved him and only him so far in her life.

If she was the cause of the breach between her father and him, and considering this latest insult in kidnapping her, she and Rob would have no possible chance now. His only choice was to expose and disavow Symon's actions as that of a renegade and turn him over to the MacLeries for their punishment and she understood that Rob would never do that. He was trying to be a good leader to his clan—as good a laird as he thought her father and his had been.

Once the servants had left and Siusan had brought her more sewing to do, she thought about the letter once more. Maybe Rob would find one of the elders who knew more about it? This day passed slowly, the noisiness outside increased from the number of people using the chambers nearby and she wondered what her father would indeed do about her.

* * *

'What happened before this letter, Murtagh?' Rob asked.

Though he would rather speak to one of the other elders, one who supported him, it turned out that Murtagh might be the only one who knew what had been going on those months ago. Now, after trying to evade speaking with him in private, the man shrugged.

'I know you think Symon should be laird and I have no problem with you having your own opinion. But I am laird now and there is a war coming to our gates. I need to know what brought that war to us.'

Rob held out a mug to the man and poured a good measure of whisky into both. Then he took the letter from the table and gave it to the counsellor. Murtagh was educated—he could read and write and even understood Latin—so Rob waited while he read it. The surprise in his eyes told Rob much.

His suspicions were correct. But he pushed now for the truth. 'Who made the first contact with the MacKenzies?'

'Well, I hate to be one to tell tales...' Murtagh

began. He paused for a mouthful of the whisky before continuing. Rob filled his cup again for good measure. 'Your da was not happy with the way the MacLerie treated you.'

Now that was a surprise. He thought that Angus and Connor remained friends until the end.

'When that...' Murtagh pointed and rolled his finger in the air '...business with the lass happened, Angus took your side. Said to wait for your explanation. That there was more to this than youthful stupidity.'

Though his father's reaction surprised him, it did nothing to explain the more recent changes.

'That is old history. More than four years ago. He remarried since then and expected an heir. Why did my father look to the MacKenzies?'

'Well, that...' Murtagh drank a large portion of his whisky and wiped his mouth with the back of his hand. 'Symon's stepda had MacKenzie ties. He thought an alliance with them would be better for us than with the MacLeries. A possible marriage was mentioned.'

Marriage? His other half-sisters from Angus's previous marriage were yet too young to enter into negotiations now. His own attempt with the

MacLerie heiress had ended in spectacular failure and he'd be no target for the MacKenzies. Could it be? 'Symon?'

'Nay, not the boy.' Murtagh shook his head. 'Tyra.'

Tyra? His now-betrothed? 'This letter and the others do not mention that at all.'

'A private arrangement, I think. First her marriage, then a stronger bond through the treaty.'

So, a gradual moving away from the MacLerie alliance to one with the MacKenzies, then? Yet neither Symon nor Tyra objected when the elders suggested instead that Rob and Tyra be joined to end the fighting between the two branches of the family.

'Did my father know of those plans? To marry her into the MacKenzies?'

'Symon's stepda talked with him about it more than a year ago, before both of their deaths. Your father did not object. Though he had hopes that Tyra would marry the MacLerie lad or Symon would wed one of Connor's kin.'

Kin or his daughter? Rob wondered.

Kidnapping was a time-honoured tradition and a means to a bride that might otherwise be out of a man's reach. Is that why Symon had kidnapped Lilidh? Once he'd taken her, did he mean to keep her? Maybe he'd thought that since Rob had rejected her once, she was available to him?

But no one here knew about Iain's death, so taking a married woman did nothing but infuriate her kin and her husband. Or had Symon known?

Rob's head spun with all the possible connections that Murtagh's words had uncovered. Like a spider's web woven across clans, each strand connected others that branched out endlessly. Who knew what when? Who wanted which clan? Why? None of that mattered in a way since in each of them was Connor's and Angus's belief that any link between their clans or with the MacKenzies would not involve the bastard son.

And, even worse, Rob becoming laird and chief had mucked things up and interfered with many plans. He had much to think about before Connor arrived at his gates, but even more to do before that happened.

'My thanks, Murtagh,' he said, slapping the man on the shoulder. 'I hope I can earn your support in the coming weeks.'

The older man blinked several times at Rob's

admission, probably not expecting to have his support requested rather than demanded. They parted then and Rob went to check on Dougal's arrangements for weapons and arrows. He prayed to God they wouldn't need them, but better to be prepared than to be found empty-handed.

By the time night had fallen, Rob believed them almost ready to deal with the MacLeries who would arrive soon. Sentries had been posted at the edges of their lands to report any sightings of anyone not invited to be there.

He had hesitated in contacting the MacKenzie laird, hoping that he and Connor could come to terms and end this peaceably. Then, with Lilidh safely returned to her parents and his clan safe from annihilation, he could decide over the future alliances that would benefit and protect his people. The fewer who were involved the better, he thought as he sat down at table for the evening meal.

Each day his hall seemed smaller as more and more from the outlying farms and the village took refuge from the coming storm there. The meals grew plainer, which suited him, though not his betrothed. Tyra wore a strange, rather self-pleased look upon her face and it gave him pause. He was growing more and more suspicious about her and her brother's roles in the débâcle he faced.

'How do you fare, Tyra?' he asked, after being served his food. He could not accuse her or Symon of anything. Yet.

'I am well,' she said with a smile. A smile that made his gut tighten with its sweetness.

'Has Symon returned yet?' he asked, glancing at the empty place next to her.

'I do not keep track of my brother's comings and goings,' she replied. He watched her face, but she gave no indication that there was another meaning or that she lied. 'Surely he carries out the duties you have assigned him, Rob.'

Rob could not resist testing her now that he was aware of other possible arrangements she'd been privy to. He took her hand in his and smiled at her.

'Once the MacLerie has his daughter back and our alliance with the MacKenzies is settled, we should set a wedding date, Tyra.'

If he had glanced away, he would never have

seen the brittle way her smile broke or the narrowing of her gaze at his words. But see them he did, so her words—when they came—had a different meaning than they would have had he not been watching her.

'It would please me to have things settled between us, Rob.'

There was much more going on here in the house of the Mathesons than he had ever imagined. But he needed to understand it before Connor got here.

The rest of the meal passed quickly. The crowded hall and heightened tension and noise had bothered Tyra, so she had asked for his leave to seek her chambers quickly. Though he suspected she did not want to risk having to speak to him about their marriage, his testing complete, he had waved his permission.

After making one more inspection of the gates and the guards posted, Rob made his way up the stairs to his chambers. He forgot for a moment about moving to another chamber and only the sight of the guards in front of his father's room reminded him.

His father's room.

Once named laird, he'd refused to move into the rooms his father had used. Thinking back now, he could not say if it was some kind of continued rebellion or that he could not accept his own worthiness to be there. Or, had he just honoured his father and did not want to live in his place?

Since others now stayed in these chambers, the guards would remain. They would patrol the corridor and the stairs from now on for any signs of trouble and to keep Lilidh safe if there was any.

'Laird,' Tomas said as he approached. 'A word before you go in.' The guard was about the same age and build as he was and they'd been friends for years. The frown that darkened his face warned Rob of something bad.

'What happened?'

'Lady Tyra was here.'

'In my chambers?' he asked.

'Nay, but she was here in one of the other rooms when Lady MacGregor was moved.'

This was not good. 'Go ahead.'

'They exchanged words and Lady Tyra slapped—'

Rob did not wait for the rest of his words, he pushed open the door and found her sitting in a chair much like the one that had been in his chambers. Her head was bowed as she scrutinised the garment she sewed. He was not quiet, charging into the room as he had, so she knew he was there.

'Lilidh.' She did not react at all, continuing to push that needle through the fabric and out again. 'Lilidh, look at me?'

Chapter Thirteen

She let out a sigh and put her hands down on her lap, the clothing lay across her legs. Then Lilidh turned her face and met his gaze. Her fair skin hid nothing and the darkening injury marred her cheek. Bruising had already begun around the edges, deep purple seeping through the reddened areas.

'No,' she said, before he could ask.

'No, I should not do this to her? Or, no, you do not think I will believe the lie when you tell me it does not hurt?' Rob approached slowly. 'If your father sees you looking like this, there is no hope for peace.'

'She is your betrothed. She is furious over my being with you.' She knew the truth about Tyra's position here—but certainly not the truth of his feelings on the matter.

'You would excuse her for doing this?'

Rob reached out and moved several loose strands of hair away from Lilidh's face, revealing the full extent of the welt. Lilidh placed her hand on his and pushed it away as she stood.

'Excuse her? No, I do not excuse her for I believe there is always a way other than force and suffering, Rob. But I understand her reaction in this. Hitting me is about the only thing she can do to show her displeasure at the insult you've committed against her honour and her pride.'

Rob stared at this extraordinary woman and wondered—not for the last time, he was certain—how things could have been between them if he had not made the choice he had. Though he had suspicions about Tyra, he had no proof and he, too, understood her reaction. Had he not done the same thing to Symon?

'I will seek no reprisal then against her,' he offered.

Lilidh nodded and turned back to sit once more. He touched her arm to stop her. Had she shivered or was his mind creating sensations that were not there?

'The tension is something that can be felt here,

Rob. And when my father arrives, it will worsen,' she offered.

Many things would worsen. If the MacLeries laid siege to his keep, many would suffer. He must come up with a way out of this. 'Would you read another document?'

Doubt flickered in her gaze, but she nodded. He went to the leather trunk that held all the papers important to the clan and found the one he wanted her to examine. With what Murtagh had told him about other possible betrothals and informal links to the MacKenzies, he thought she might find something he'd missed in his review of it.

'Would you walk with me?' Rob asked her after a short time had passed. 'I would rather not discuss this here.' He glanced at the door and the now-noisy corridor filled with the elders and others returning to their chambers for the night from the hall.

He found her cloak, the one his men had recovered along with her other garments from the wreckage of her travelling party's cart, and placed it on her shoulders, barely controlling his need to touch her face. They made their way up to the battlements and walked the perimeter once, giving her time to loosen the muscles in her legs and a reprieve, he knew, from being inside the entire day and night. When they reached the base of the ruined tower, Rob stopped and turned to her, blocking the worst of the winds with his body. Then he explained what Murtagh had revealed. Her surprise at any marriage connection being discussed with her family told him that the MacLeries might not be as interested in such a bond as perhaps his father or cousin was. And, now, with his daughter's mistreatment at his hands, Rob doubted Connor would ever approve or allow Lilidh to remain here as any Matheson's wife or connect their families in any other way.

Their discussion over, Rob held out his arm to escort Lilidh back down the stairs to his chamber, but she shook her head.

'May I stay a few more minutes? The fresh air clears my head.'

He nodded and went to speak to the men on guard. There was no doubt that the MacLeries would arrive soon and he wanted everyone watchful for signs of any outriders from their main force. Even as he talked to the men, his

gaze never left Lilidh. She made her way back
to the edge of the battlements and stared out into
the forest surrounding the keep. Her home, Lairig
Dubh, was to the south and east of Keppoch,
the MacGregors to the north and east. Then she
leaned her head back and closed her eyes. Reaching out, she rested her hands on the stone wall
and just remained in that position for some minutes. Just as he was about to go back to her, she
opened her eyes, leaned her head forwards and
turned to face him.

As he approached, she never looked away. Her
eyes filled with the same desire that he'd witnessed when she'd awoken from that dream in
his bed. But she was not sleeping this time and he
could not tell if she was thinking about Iain now
or not. A thought crept into his mind then—if
and how could a depth of emotion be created between a man and a woman in the short time she'd
been married to the MacGregor? The stabbing
fire of jealousy tore into his own heart then as he
realised how much he'd allowed to slip through
his hands.

By being weak.

By being afraid.

By not being worthy.

When he stood before her, her gaze fell to his mouth and his to hers. The wanting had never ceased for him, never lessened even though he'd agreed to do what Connor wanted of him—repudiate Lilidh and leave. There wasn't a day he did not think of her or grieve over his actions.

Or want her.

So, he took the last step between them and touched his mouth to hers. Her lips softened under his and she did not move away. He raised his hand up and cupped her head, holding her there, though only just. Rob tilted his face and kissed her again. This time she opened her mouth for him as she did in their times together. He was not certain if she'd forgiven him for the past, but she had not forgotten. She had not forgotten him.

He felt her hands grasp his jacket and his body heated at the way her fingers tickled him as she tried to hold on to him. Once she had hold of him, she pulled him closer. The soft touch of the tip of her tongue on his startled and pleased him. He let her explore his mouth for a few glorious moments and then he could not hold back, taking possession of her mouth as he'd dreamt of doing these last four years.

This kiss was not the same as the one in the hall when she was brought here. That one was for show and ended in anger. This one—well, this one simply demanded another and another until they were both breathless. He lifted his mouth from hers and leaned back, his hand yet tangled in her hair and keeping her head close.

'I want you, Lilidh,' he whispered. 'I have always wanted you.'

He touched his lips to hers again, barely for a moment, and then he stepped back, lest he toss her to the ground and have the rest of her right here, right now. He could have held his control had she not been so soft beneath him. If she had not taken hold of him and drawn him closer. He had almost escaped her effect on him, but then she spoke, whispered, a reply.

'And I want you, Rob Matheson.'

Where the wanton had hidden for these last four years, she knew not, but when his mouth touched hers it was back in full force. Her body heated and blood raced and places deep within grew heavy in anticipation of what came next. As during the times they'd loved, during their secret encounters, her body did not care if his touch was wrong, it simply wanted.

It wanted him and the sensual magic he could create within her as he caressed and pleasured her in ways she'd never dreamt of. Her breasts ached and the tips of them tightened, tingling in hope that he would touch her there, again, soon.

If she was to leave here and be given to someone else in marriage, she would not go without finishing what she and Rob had started all those years ago. No one expected her to be a virgin bride after her first marriage, so that would not make or break negotiations for a future match. If she had the opportunity to choose the man to whom she would give herself to, and if fate now provided her that chance for its own strange reasons, she would seize it.

Knowing that Rob had not ordered her kidnapping and that he sought to protect his people and not take the easiest way out also made her understand that he would never force himself on her now. He could have any night in his bed if that had been his plan. A man who would force a woman would not care if she was awake or asleep. He would not care if her leg hurt and could not walk the steps. He would not care if she were being mistreated.

Rob cared. Rob made certain of her safety and comfort and even allowed her this measure of freedom or time alone here where it gave her pleasure. He tried to protect her against his own kin.

If nothing else, allowing this thing to happen between them, this unexpressed passion that remained between them, even after their terrible parting and the hurt that took years to burn away, would give her the closure she needed before moving on in her life. Perhaps, if she'd not seen him again, she would not feel this way. Alas, she had and she did.

But the wanton within reminded her that mostly she just wanted to experience the full measure of passion that had been promised her in their beginnings. Her body wanted to take that final step with Rob and no other.

To prove her words, to herself and to him, she lifted up on her toes and, taking his head in her hands, drew his mouth down to her. This time she explored his mouth, using the tip of her tongue to outline his firm lips. When he opened, she tasted all that he was. Rob moved closer, lifting his cloak open and wrapping it and his arms around her. His body was all hardened muscles and she felt safe. He made her feel that way. Then, the sound of shuffling feet made her pull back.

She had completely forgotten the guards. She'd forgotten they stood on top of the battlements of his keep. She'd forgotten herself. Rob kept her wrapped in his cloak as the guards passed them on their rounds, so she did not have to acknowledge them. Lilidh pulled free once they'd passed and were far enough away not to hear their words.

'Have you changed your mind, then?' Rob asked as he watched her with eyes filled with desire. She smiled at him, for she heard the undercurrent of worry in his voice as he asked.

'No,' she said, shaking her head. She had not. 'But it is cold here and I prefer no witnesses to what happens between us.'

It was not as though every person living or staying in Keppoch Keep did not already think them lovers. Or think that Rob had not taken advantage of her favours while sleeping in his bed together. Most of them even believed his hard use of her the cause for her limp. Somehow, though, she suddenly felt shy about letting them see that it was real.

She lost her breath in the next moment as he bent over, lifted her into his arms and carried her to the doorway. Lilidh encircled his neck with her arms, but he held her securely as he made his way down the steps towards his chamber. She tucked her head down against him as he waited for one of the guards to open the door. A smile played on her mouth as Tomas asked if she was well.

The slammed door in his face was the only answer Rob gave. A hearty laugh echoed across the chamber as Tomas gave his reply.

'Are you well?' Rob asked as he let her feet touch the floor. 'Your face?'

'Does not pain me,' she said as she allowed Rob to remove her cloak and toss it aside. Now inside, now that the moment was nigh, her nerves struck.

He'd refused to marry her because of the damage to her leg four years ago. Would it diminish the desire he felt for her now? How would he react to the sight of it when they joined?'

'But something worries you,' he said, lifting wind-loosened hair out of her face and lifting her chin so he could look at her. He winced and she knew the various bumps and bruises were quite visible now. 'We can stop now. It is your choice.'

'I thought I was a prisoner without choice?' she asked.

'You are a prisoner. But in this matter between us, you have but to say the word and I will not.'

Did she want this? Truly? Looking at him now, knowing that everything would change as soon as her family arrived and that she would never get this chance again...

Yes, she did.

'Which things will you not do, Rob?' she asked coyly.

He'd whispered wicked promises to her as he touched her and stroked her body those times before. Now she wanted to hear those promises once more and she wanted to feel all that she should have—so she would have the memories of it when she left.

Her body filled with a sense of anticipation as he walked behind her and stood so close they almost touched. She could feel his breath on her neck and he untied the strips holding her hair into a thick plait and unravelled the length of it. The movement of his fingers as they slid over her scalp and into the tresses, separating and then mixing the strands all the way down to its ends tickled and excited her. Rob avoided touching her injury, yet seemed to massage every inch of her head.

He lifted the length of her hair to one side and touched his mouth to her neck there. Shivers shot through her at the warmth of his mouth. Then he leaned her head away and kissed the cord of muscle between her head and shoulders, making her gasp at its sensitivity.

'I think I should just learn your body before we do more,' he said in a husky whisper. She felt her body ready itself for his attention, which she hoped would be soon.

Then he moved his hand across her, gently touching her before coming to rest on her breast. Pulling her back against him, he cupped the fullness of her and flicked his thumb over that sensitive nipple. She arched against him, against that part of him that had come to life between their bodies. With her trapped under his arm, he bit her neck then, gently along that delicate cord until she gasped over and over.

When he slipped his other hand around to rest on her hip and then caress her thigh, she let go and leaned against him fully, allowing him to touch where he would. Her head fell back on his shoulder and his breath grew ragged against her ear as he continued to touch her. Her hands fell to her side and in a bold move, she placed them on his legs, revelling in the firmness and strength of his body. He moved then, the proof of his arousal hard against her, hissing in a sharp breath.

Then, just as her body urged her to completely surrender, the fear took hold and she pulled away from him. Breathing hard, she turned to face him, for she needed to see his eyes when she asked that question that plagued and terrified her.

'Is this just another way to shame me, Rob? Will you use my desire against me as you did before?'

She took in a breath and let it out quickly, pushing out the real question as fast as she could before she lost courage. For under it all, the humiliation she'd suffered due to his cruel words and rejection was something she did not think she would survive again.

'If you did not want me before, and because of my leg, how can you want me now?'

Chapter Fourteen

He stood looking into the damage he'd wrought to her with his cruel and unforgivable words. The vibrant spirit had been crushed. The girl he'd loved had been killed by his actions and this woman carried the injury to her heart and her spirit even more than the damage to her leg. Rob rubbed his face and pushed his hair back as he gazed into her eyes.

'You think I will use your willingness against you? That this is just a ploy to hurt you, again?'

What else could she think? Though he'd not ordered her brought there or mistreated, he'd allowed it. The last time they'd met alone, he'd left her to seek out her father for permission to marry her. Instead of returning to her with words of love and promises for a future together, he'd broken things with her in front of her family and used her leg, her 'maimed and disgusting leg', as his excuse. He wanted perfection in his bride, he'd said, and when he'd discovered how bad it truly was—during some scandalous mischief alone with her—he knew he could not stomach nights with her in his bed.

God damn him to hell! Regardless of the weakness within him that allowed him to say such terrible things, the effects of them could still be seen in the fear in her eyes. Not for any physical act that would happen between them, nay, but for the possibility of him tearing her heart and spirit apart once more.

No matter that her father had insisted that he repudiate her in the worst way so that there was no hope of reconciliation, he should have stood up to Connor and refused. He should have demanded Lilidh as his wife, laird—father—earl be damned!

Instead he'd let the man he respected and admired, the man who'd trained him as warrior and mentored him as a leader, force him into actions that had destroyed both of their lives. The only thing he had left her with was her love for her father, for he had not and would never admit to her that they would have been together if not for Connor MacLerie's demands and orders.

Looking now into her eyes, eyes filled with desire and hope and fear, he could still not destroy the love she bore Connor.

'Lilidh, I was a stupid boy, full of himself with no idea how to handle things like love. Or a woman's heart,' he admitted now. 'I have learned much in these last year so that matters that seemed so important then are not now.'

He took her hands in his and held them. He must ease her fears, for he had no intention of allowing this chance to make the past up to her to be lost. It had nothing to do with shaming her before his clan—it had to do with restoring her confidence and showing that he was the unworthy one and not her.

'This is between us. I will not speak of whatever happens between us with anyone else. And I will not force you to my bed or take that which you do not freely give.'

Though doubt filled those deep-green eyes, he watched as she made the decision. No matter what, he would do whatever he needed to do to keep her safe, pay whatever price he owed at whatever cost it was to him, to make up for what he'd done to her.

When she pulled her hands from his and began unbuckling his jacket, he knew she'd made up her mind to trust him and he let out the breath he did not know he held. He dropped his arms to his side and allowed her to do whatever she wanted. After opening the jacket and pushing it down off his shoulders, she went to work untying the laces of his shirt and tugging it off over his head.

The touch of her fingers on his skin nearly caused his knees to give out. She outlined his ribs and then used both hands across him, touching him as he had done to her. He fought the overwhelming urge to let loose his control and to show her all the pleasure now. He held still as her fingers traced lower and lower and reached his belt. With nary a pause, she tugged on the belt until it came free and then let it and the tartan it held in place fall to the floor around their feet.

He had always been the leader, taking her through the first steps in their intimate dance, but it pleased him now to allow her to have her way. He closed his eyes and gave himself over to whatever she wanted to do—a benefit of making love to a woman of experience rather than a virgin.

Her hands followed the hair on his belly down further and further until she reached his manhood. Standing thick and firm, it jutted out from the curls at its base and the expression on her face, a mix of interest and hunger, made it pulse and move. He waited for her to touch him there and it was worth every moment of the four years since he'd last laid eyes on her. She slid her gentle hands over and around it, taking hold and then stroking the length of it. Then she lifted his bollocks in her grasp, caressing them together.

He thought he was dying then. His blood rushed so fast and hard through every part of him that it hurt to take a breath. His skin burned. His hands itched to touch her. And he would, all in good time. For now, he let her roam over his body, accepting the exquisite torture of it.

But when she bent over and moved that mouth of hers closer to his aroused flesh, he took her by the shoulders and straightened her back up. Her mouth on his cock. He needed to be lying down or he would fall over at such a thing.

So he kissed her and began to untie and undo the various layers she wore, touching and caressing her body as he did. He let his hand linger on her breast and he untied the laces of her gown. He let his finger graze over the curls at the juncture of her legs. He touched and tasted her skin as he uncovered her bit by bit. When he felt her tremble beneath each caress, he knew she was ready.

Reaching down, he took the edge of her shift and began to lift it up. Anxious to hold her naked, with nothing between them, her hand on his surprised him. Ah. She did not want him to see her leg, no matter his words that it mattered not. He let the garment go—there were ways to deal with it—and lifted her into his arms to carry her to bed. Rob laid her down and climbed in next to her, kissing her mouth and keeping the fires of passion stoked within her.

Not allowing the thin shift to slow or stop him, he kissed her breasts through it until she arched beneath him. The heat pulsed through him at her reaction, his body demanding that he take her soon. Instead, determined that this was for her, he turned his attentions to her other breast, suckling the tight bud this time. She gasped and stiffened under him.

Kneeling over her, he slid down her, using his face and mouth and teeth to tease a path towards the place he wanted to taste. The fabric was no barrier to what she felt, for her breathing became erratic and when he placed his head on her stomach, he felt the pounding of her heart. He slid down a bit and moved his mouth over the curls there, just once, but she let out a moan and so he used his tongue to tease them over and over. When her legs fell open, he moved his face down and kissed the uninjured thigh, easing his way towards his goal—the place that would make her soar in pleasure.

At first, she urged him on with her hands tangled in his hair, but then they fell aside and her fingers curled in the bedcovers. Her hips urged him on that way.

'Take it off,' she rasped out then.

Rob raised his head to make sure he'd heard her correctly. 'Your shift?'

'Yes.'

He would not waste time now so he grasped the top edges of the garment and ripped it open. Her lovely body lay open to his view, her soft curves making his mouth water once more. Although it had been a big step for her, he did not want her uncomfortable during this, so he tucked the now-freed edge around her scarred leg, giving her a measure of privacy in that.

The rest of her was more spectacular now than before—her body had matured into a lithe, curvaceous woman from the girl he'd known. He'd adored her then—he loved her now.

Lifting her uninjured leg up and over, he opened that most sensitive place to his gaze. Kissing down from her knee, along her thigh, he finally placed his mouth where it wanted to be and she moaned out a sound of hunger and longing and pleasure. Rob tasted her arousal, until she panted, barely a moment or two away from reaching satisfaction. He plunged his tongue deep and sent her over the edge. Her body pressed against him, her hands tangled again in his hair, but he did not stop until she throbbed.

She pulled his hair then, dragging him up to face her, their bodies sliding along each other and letting her know that they were not done yet.

Lilidh's eyes were wild, filled with pleasure and desire when she gazed at him.

'Now, Rob,' she urged. 'Finish it.'

Lilidh's body sung, from his touch and from the scandalous kisses between her legs. She was ready for the next step—she wanted it, wanted him. Inside.

Inside where no man had ever been.

Rob moved over her, once more working his magic as he sent her body into another needy frenzy. Her hips lifted, begging him to fill her. Her breasts, heavy and aching, needed him inside her to ease the building tension. Her very core throbbed in anticipation of having his flesh within hers, touching her there, joining their bodies as one.

He moved slowly, tasting his way along her body, until she was ready to beg him.

Nay, she would beg.

'Please, Rob,' she whispered. 'Please.' When he placed his erection at the opening to her most intimate place, she held her breath and waited that incredibly small amount of time before he began to push inside her.

Would he notice? Would he know? Did it matter to him?

As he moved in, pressing deeper, he paused and looked at her. She met his gaze and saw the question there. Holding her breath, she arched and lifted her hips, seating him deeply within her aching flesh. Then, for a moment, she could not tell where he ended and she began. Closing her eyes, she revelled in the feeling of joining with him.

It was all that she'd imagined and dreamt it would be.

'Lilidh?' Rob asked. She opened her eyes and met his beautiful blue gaze. 'Are you well?'

'I am.' There had been only some tightness, but that eased with each moment he remained inside of her.

'You should have told me.'

Did he regret this already, then? Tears began to burn in her eyes and in her throat. His mouth on hers was a surprise.

'I would have had a care for you, my love.' He kissed her lips and chin and then her neck. The touches inflamed her body once more and she felt him lengthen and thicken inside her.

She thought he would withdraw, but instead he began to move, slowly at first, drawing out a bit and then sliding back in. Then he moved faster, pulling back and plunging until he could go no further. Her flesh clung to his, creating an exhilarating tension there and all through her. The same excitement he'd caused before, but this time so much more intense. Her heart pounded and her blood boiled as he thrust over and over, bringing her to that edge once again.

Lilidh grabbed his hips and pressed against him, urging him to the same edge and then she felt all the tension and tightness inside of her release. She gasped as their bodies pulsed together.

It was some moments before she came back to herself after such an experience. She lay still, enjoying the closeness of him.

A few seconds or minutes passed before he moved. Slowly he withdrew from her, leaving her feeling empty in a place that she'd never known could be. Lilidh knew a reckoning was coming and she dreaded facing him, now that he knew of her deceit. His actions surprised her instead.

She watched as he silently left the bed and gathered some things together before returning. A basin, some hot water from the pot on the hearth, cloths, a cup of wine. He carried them back to the bed and, after pulling the bedcovers and torn shift from under her, he first handed her the wine. Its sweet flavour eased the dryness in her throat as she sipped it.

Then dipped a cloth in the hot water and cleaned himself...of her virgin's blood. The next cloth he offered to her and she accepted it, handing him the wine, and cleaned the signs of their joining—and her first—from between her legs. Using the ruined shift as a drying cloth she finished as quickly as she could.

Her body felt heavy everywhere and when he climbed back next to her in the bed and pulled her to his side, she moulded to his body. Surrounded by his arms, warmed by his heat and the layers of blankets and eased by the wine, she found herself drifting into sleep.

Rob watched as her eyelids fluttered once and then twice before shutting altogether. Her body lay against him, skin to skin now, and she gave herself over to sleep much as she'd given herself to him.

Totally.

He was just as stunned now as when he'd felt the thin barrier inside her as he'd claimed her. He'd had no idea of how complete that claiming would be.

First. Her first. No one, no other man, had enjoyed her body since last they'd been together. He'd been saving that special joining until their marriage. He'd expected that, with her marriage to Iain, her virginity would have been taken by that man.

So, how was she yet untouched? Why had her husband not claimed his marital rights? He smoothed the hair from her face and studied the arch of her brow, the curve of her chin. He eased his arm out from under her and drew the covers higher around her shoulders. Lilidh turned on to her other side and sighed in her sleep.

Rob climbed from the bed and found more wine. Filling a cup, he walked to one of the two windows in the chamber and stared out into the darkness.

Lilidh a virgin?

He swallowed deeply from the cup and considered how a thing would have been possible.

Had Iain been ill during their marriage? Hell, Rob would have had to be dead before he would neglect her as his wife. Yet, clearly Iain had not.

If you did not want me before because of my leg, how can you want me now?

The question she'd asked him gave him pause now. Had her injury presented such an obstacle to her new husband that he did not bed her because of it?

Daft man, then. But had she told her parents of her marriage's failure? Was that why she returned home? Did anyone know the truth?

But now he'd not only taken her virginity, he'd spilled his seed within her. That changed everything...or did it? In the way in which this whole situation would play out over the coming weeks? He just did not know. Did it make him want to claim her and keep her? He wanted to scream out the words now.

But could he? Chances were that the most likely outcome would be Lilidh's return to her family and his alliance with the MacKenzies—hopefully without losing too many of his kin. The worst? Well, his clan dead and decimated and his body hung in pieces on his wall as a warning to others not to cross the MacLerie.

She stirred in his bed, *in his bed where he'd always dreamt of having her*, so he finished the wine and went back to her. As he moved behind her and drew her close, his body reacted. Instead of waking, she just wiggled back against him, nestling beside him.

Rob had many questions to ask and things to think about, but when the dawn came, he was no closer to resolution than before. Lilidh slept through the knock on the door and never moved as he left. His questions would have to wait until this night.

Chapter Fifteen

Lilidh heard the knocking on the door, but her body resisted the call to wake. As she pushed the covers back, she discovered herself completely naked. She tried to gather her hair into a neat queue, but it was wildly loose all around her shoulders. Sliding to the side of the bed, she glanced around for something to use as a bedrobe. Finding none, she pulled her gown over her head and tugged it into place.

Before she could find the brush needed to conquer the tangles in her hair, the door opened and Beathas led a cadre of servants in behind her. Two men rolled in the wooden tub and placed it near the hearth. In this bigger chamber, there was more room to move around it. Buckets of steaming water followed. Other bathing supplies as well as bedclothes were delivered before everyone turned and left—except for Beathas, who stood by the door giving her a very knowing look.

'Let me check your head, dearie,' Beathas said as she walked over to Lilidh. 'Rob said it might have been bleeding last night.'

Bleeding? Her head had not bled...

But that would explain away any signs of blood on the bed, if any was there. So she sat and let Beathas have her look.

'The stitches look fine, but they will need to come out soon,' the woman declared, still watching her with a strange expression. 'Here, now, let me help you into the bath. Rob was quite insistent that you have one this morn.'

'I can manage on my own, Beathas,' she said, rising from the chair where she sat and walking over to the tub. She turned back to dismiss the woman when she found her frowning.

'Did no one ever see to you, lass? I've seen your leg, so there's no reason to try to hide it from me.'

Ah. When she was unconscious. She should have known.

'Did Rob also see it?' she asked. Beathas tsked as she moved around the chamber, gathering up dirty clothing that needed washing and pulling the used sheets from the bed.

'Anyone who has seen the injuries of a battle would think it tame in comparing it.'

'Only Isla has seen it recently. Before that the healer and my parents when it happened. 'Tis not something I wish to show others.' If her tone was a bit sharp, surely Beathas would understand the private nature of her injury.

'Isla is your maid?' Beathas asked. Walking towards her, the older woman motioned towards the gown she wore and Lilidh nodded allowing her approach.

'Twas true. The healer had seen her leg before so there was no use or purpose to be gained by hiding it from her. And having help in her bath would be a luxury. She stood as the woman lifted the gown off and then held her steady as she climbed into the tub. Sliding down, she noticed that the soreness in her leg was not the only one in her body.

'She was. Until she was killed when Symon attacked me.' It simply did not feel real to her that Isla could be gone.

The woman continued to help her wash, untangle her hair and see to her needs.

Some time later, as Lilidh sat by the fire dressed and brushing her hair out, there was a quick knock on the door and it opened. Rob walked in and she waited to see if matters between them had changed now that he knew her truth.

'Can you come down to the kitchens?' he asked. 'There is something I think you should see.'

He stood with his hand out to her and she could not tell much from his expression or words. Knowing her difficulties with the stairs, he would not have asked this of her on a whim. Beathas handed her a plaid shawl and she followed Rob to the steps. It took some time, but he did not rush her at all. When they reached the main floor, he waited for her catch her breath.

'I should have ordered the bath after you did this,' he offered, smiling at her.

'No, I had a good long soak and it feels fine.'

She wondered if he would speak of more intimate issues between them. They walked in silence, though he let her walk on her own as they passed through the great hall and headed for the kitchens. This was much different from the last time she walked this path. Though there were many within the hall, none seemed to bother with her for now. Escorted by Rob, she made her way into the kitchen area where Siusan stood waiting.

'Am I to work here again?' she asked, uncertain about what was his plan in this.

'No,' he answered as they followed Siusan down a smaller corridor to the chamber at the end.

Siusan opened the door and allowed them to enter. Although neither had said anything alarming, Lilidh held her breath as she walked into the chamber. There, on a small pallet, rested an older woman. Isla?

It could not be!

But it was her and she lay with her eyes closed. Lilidh stumbled over to her side, taking her hand and whispering her name over and over until her maid opened her eyes and met her gaze.

'Isla. I am gladdened to see you alive,' she said. 'How do you feel?'

'A bit weak, my lady,' she whispered. 'But I wi' be on my feet and takin' care of you soon, I promise.'

'Hush now, you rest and recover, Isla. I am fine.'

She closed her eyes once more and seemed to fall into a deep sleep then, but Lilidh could not let go of her hand. Glancing around through the tears that now filled her own eyes, she found Rob watching her from the doorway. 'I thought her dead.'

'I know. And until just this morn when Beathas declared her strong enough to live, we thought she would not survive.' Rob walked to her side. 'I did not want you to mourn twice if you did not need to,' he said softly against her ear.

She nodded her head because words were not possible at that moment.

'You may remain with her until nightfall. Call a guard if you need to return to my chambers before that,' he instructed.

Lilidh turned to thank him, but he'd gone and only Siusan remained. 'How long has she been here?'

'They found her the day after you were brought here. A wound to her head, much like yours.'

'And you have been caring for her?' Lilidh asked.

'Some of the women, too,' Siusan replied.

'I will sit with her now,' she offered. 'Is there anything I should know about her care?'

Siusan pointed out several items, a concoction left by Beathas as well as fresh bandages if she had need of them, and then left her with instructions to keep the door closed at all times. Something she'd not noticed before—a tray of food along with broth for Isla—also waited for her to break her fast. Nodding her understanding, Lilidh watched as Siusan left.

She pulled a stool over and rearranged the table that held the food and supplies so she could reach everything and still touch Isla's hand. She ate and watched the rise and fall of her maid's chest. At least she lived. When her father arrived, she would try to convince Rob to let the woman go home to Lairig Dubh.

The day was moving slowly, all the while memories of the night before kept seeping into her thoughts. She relived it all in her mind, every touch, every kiss, everything. A good thing no one else was there and watching or they would wonder at the constant blush on her face. The wanton had had her way and was satisfied by what had happened between her and Rob. But what now? What came next?

Siusan returned from time to time with clothing to mend and small tasks she could do while at Isla's side. She spoke to her maid, though she was unsure if she heard anything throughout the day. Isla roused several times, mumbled a few words and then slept again. When the noises from the kitchens grew louder, she knew it was nearing nightfall as they finished the work on the evening meal.

And time to return to Rob's chambers.

How would it be between them now? Would he demand the truth from her? She guessed that a man liked to know if he was or was not a woman's first, but did it matter now?

As she waited for the guard, she thought on her own feelings about this. It had been thrilling. More pleasure than she could have guessed could happen. She knew how a man and woman joined, but the way he used his mouth on her was a shock to her. Who could have thought something like that possible? Her body shivered then, reminding her of just how wonderful it had been between them.

Was that to be the end of it, then?

She'd convinced herself to take advantage of the chance to be with him before this was over, but what now? Should she seek out the small lonely bed in the laird's chamber and retain what little of her honour she could? Or should she live as she wished to as long as this fantasy existed and go back to her real life with enough memories to last for her whole life long?

First she must speak to Rob, but how could she admit to him that her husband found her so displeasing he could not consummate their vows? Though men would ignore much for a bit of bedplay, apparently as her father had warned her, Iain MacGregor could not. So, she had borne the shame alone until now. How could she even admit such a thing aloud to him? Would he ask?

She bade Isla farewell and left her in the care of a young servant girl for the night. Lilidh hoped Rob would permit her to return on the morrow. The guard must have be given orders, for his pace was slow as they made their way down the corridor, through the kitchens and out a different door that would have them go around the hall. Since she wanted no more interactions with Tyra, she was glad of it.

But, just before they turned to go up the stairs, she peered into the entry of the hall and saw Rob sitting at the high table with only Tyra. Symon was not to be seen. The hall was filled so there was no way he could hear her. He turned his head at just that moment and their gazes met. Even from this distance she could feel or read the desire in his for her. She shivered so much, in anticipation, in remembering, that the guard reached out to steady her.

Wrapping the shawl around her shoulders, she followed him up the stairs to wait on Rob's return...and all that meant for them this night.

Tyra followed his gaze. Not that she needed to in order to know what he looked at—or rather, who. She knew the slut stood at the back of the hall from the way his eyes softened and stared. He'd stopped with his hand halfway to his mouth, like the village idiot unable to feed himself. He seemed to gather his wits and realise what he must look like, for he coughed and put the bread down and lifted his cup instead.

She took a deep breath and let it out, exhausted now from hours of waiting for him to punish her for disobeying his orders. Nothing could be clearer than his order that the MacLerie woman was his and no one was to touch her. Though she imagined it was like a dog marking his territory against incursion, she did not fool herself into believing that her striking the bitch was not disobeying him.

So, she prepared herself all day for the summons or the angry interruption from him. Laird Rob Matheson. She understood power—its uses and misuses. She understood that she'd overstepped the boundaries he'd set around his little bedmate. She understood after living with a father who did not allow anyone to disobey his word, or punishment would follow for that defiance.

She would hold Rob to the same standard to which she held her father and her brother—if he hit her, he'd better kill her or she would be the last one standing. Her father had laughed at her bold words, but she was here and he was under the dirt in the burial grounds next to the chapel. Her brother tended to think he was in charge and she let him think that—it was easier to control and guide him that way. The fool!

Now, it was Rob's turn.

So, when he greeted her attendance at his table with a warm smile, chills ran down her back. The smile and soft tone worried her more than when her father would rant and rail. His gentle touch on her shoulder as he passed by her to his chair made gooseflesh rise on her skin. Dinner became a tense time as she waited for him to lash out at her.

Since every living person within Keppoch Keep knew she'd struck Lilidh MacLerie, it would stand to reason that he would retaliate in public so that all could witness. It's what men of power did. Against her will, Tyra became skittish. Every time he lifted his hand, she braced. Each time he turned his attention to her, she waited for his harsh words and threats.

And the meal went on in peace. The conversation pleasant especially since her brother who tended to be sulky and bitter was absent.

Now, he sat there with a stupid grin on his face,

watching the girl climb the steps to his chambers. She probably should feel some gratitude that the MacLerie's daughter was the target of his lust and she was not. As his betrothed, no one would nay-say his rights to her even before the vows were spoken. Indeed, many betrothed anticipated their vows often. Her own mother was carrying her at the wedding to her father.

If he had chosen to take her to his bed in these months before their wedding, no one would have questioned him. That he instead chose to rut Lilidh MacLerie like she was a bitch in heat was a good thing in her estimation. It made her life easier and allowed her time and caused enough distraction to him for her to put her plans in place.

So, she allowed herself a momentary victory of a sort—she'd not been reprimanded or even questioned about the incident with Lilidh this morning. Letting out her breath for the first time all day, the shock of his words and tone caught her by surprise.

'You seem to think my orders do not apply to you, lady, but they do. Most certainly,' he said in a low voice that did not carry past their table. He leaned in towards her, a smile on his features that was as false as the one usually on hers. 'If you go near her, if you send someone to her, if you speak of or to her, I will get rid of you once and for all.'

Though part of her wanted to laugh as if he jested, another part of her deep inside grew alarmed by his demeanour. She waited now for the blow, more nervous than she'd ever been.

'Do you understand my words, Tyra?' he asked, his voice softer and more menacing than before.

Fearful that she might cry out, she could only shake her head in reply. He accepted it and leaned back in his chair.

'Goodnight then, lady,' he said so that all could hear. 'Seek your bed and I wish you fair dreams.'

Tyra forced a smile on her face as she stood. She did not make the mistake of taking her gaze off him as she curtsied low and then turned to leave.

Once back in her chambers, she dismissed her maids and readied herself for bed. And she planned her next steps. Symon had almost accepted the bastard's offer of friendship and a place at his board. The fool would accept the scraps, but she would not.

Distrust would provide a powerful weapon to keep the two apart. Tyra knew what she needed to do. Arrangements were already in place. Executing the next part of her plan would be relatively easy.

Executing, she thought. Laughing at the word, she fell asleep easily that night.

Lairig Dubh

Connor stood and watched over the yard from his favourite place high on the walls. It was the place where Jocelyn would wait for him and where they spent many pleasurable moments. Now, he remained here and reconsidered his plan—something he did not do well or often. After sending Rurik, Duncan and Jocelyn to Keppoch to get Lilidh back, he wondered if the sins of his past were coming back to haunt him.

Obsessed would be a better word, for he had lost several nights of sleep over the last week. Part of him wondered if he'd made the right decision in forcing his foster son to disavow his love for Lilidh and leave. Part wondered if, in failing to rise to his challenge, Rob had indeed proven himself unworthy as he thought he was. And a deeper part had thought and hoped that Rob would have defied his edict and claimed Lilidh. Now, it seemed that the fates laughed at him once more as he must intervene again between Rob and Lilidh.

The one thing that truly plagued him was that Rob had done this simply to get Lilidh back. And to prove he could and would best the Beast in a contest of wills and abilities.

Was this all about Lilidh, then? Rob had not indicated any interest in her in the years since his departure. Not when matches for her hand were being considered. Not when the first talk of ending the alliance between their clans began and not even now. The demand received was gold for her safe return. No offer of marriage.

So, it would seem that Rob was not worthy of his daughter—not now, not then. Or was he?

Connor let the winds buffet him as he thought about the matter. The moon had risen high in the sky when he stepped from the shelter of the alcove and called out to one of the men below.

This was more than clan against clan—this was

a personal matter between him and his foster son and one that he must deal with face to face. He gathered his commanders and made plans to go to Keppoch.

And he would take enough men to finish this once and for all.

Chapter Sixteen

Lilidh glanced at the door for the hundredth time since her return. Nervousness raced in her veins as she waited for Rob's arrival. How would he confront her about her virginity? Would they be lovers again this night?

From his words, she knew that decision was up to her.

And from the way her body felt right now— arousal and excitement pulsing through her, a slow and easy throbbing in all the places he'd touched last night—she wanted him again.

More than before.

Her perceptions about what could exist between them had been based on her naïve knowledge and hearing of tales, but now her body understood the call of this intimate experience. And the promise of more.

Shaking herself free of the ever-increasing longing within her, Lilidh decided to take a look at another document for clues about how things went so badly between her father and Rob's. After discovering where the servants had moved things to in this much-larger chamber, she settled at the table and began reading some of the older documents—letters between their fathers.

Thinking back to what had happened, Lilidh tried to piece the events together and compare them to the letters. Nothing explicit in the letters explained the circumstances—Rob's request for her hand or his shaming disavowal of their love—but those kinds of details would not be for these letters, which could and would be read by others. Many nobles and chiefs and lairds did not read, so their communications were read to them by clerks or others.

Still, even the gradual increase in hostility in these letters did not feel right to her. Rob said his youthful stupidity was to blame for his actions. If that was true, why did her father refer to other matters between them in sending Rob back to his father? Why did Rob's father not question it?

Digging deeper into the box, she discovered a

small parchment, folded and undisturbed. Tucked inside another as it was, she almost missed it. Opening it—the seal had already been broken—Lilidh discovered that it was addressed to Rob, not the laird.

And it was from her mother!

Why had her mother contacted Rob? From the date, she realised it was not long ago. Just before her betrothal to Iain MacGregor was finalised. Reading on, Lilidh felt her mouth drop open at its content.

One sentence long—*My husband is about to formally accept Iain MacGregor's suit for Lilidh's hand in marriage.*

Nothing else but her mother's signature, written in her own hand, which Lilidh recognised.

Lilidh leaned back against the chair and considered the significance of this missive. Although no opinion was given, it was clear that her mother was questioning the match. Why else send something like this? And that she let Rob know of it after four years' separation and an ugly ending was stranger still.

Her heart sank as she also realised that Rob had known about her coming marriage and done nothing. Her mother had given him an opportunity to address the situation—matured and past his youthful stupidity, as he'd called it—and he had chosen to do nothing about it.

Laying it aside for now, she continued to look through the other letters there, hoping for some explanation. Certainly these were only one half of the story—her father's replies and opinions—and she had no way of knowing what Laird Matheson had written or written back...

After reading several of them, all she knew was that something more had happened between Rob and her father to cause this breach. His father clearly stood behind him, illegitimate or not, but he viewed this as a personal matter and not one to bring their clan loyalties into play.

So, how and why had it led to the clans breaking their alliance?

The footsteps coming down the corridor and the sound of his deep voice speaking to the guards ended all thought about letters and contracts, though she was able to slip the letter from her mother into her gown before losing the ability to think completely. For each second that passed before the latch lifted, her body readied for him.

If she thought what had happened between them would be once for memory's sake, she knew now she was wrong.

She wanted him for as long as she could have him.

Even as his prisoner.

Even with no promises past this time together.

No matter the outcome—she wanted him.

Lilidh stood as Rob pushed open the door; the hairs on the back of her neck tingled as did her breasts as she watched him enter. Her breath caught as their eyes met and he smiled at her.

'Good evening, Lilidh,' he said, as he closed the door behind him. 'How do you fare?'

'You sent someone to look for Isla that day?' He took a step closer and her breath stopped.

'Aye. I hoped Symon had not...' He paused then and gave her a strange look. 'Are you well?' Another step closer and her body ached.

'Well?' Her thoughts scattered as her mind filled with memories of his mouth, his hands, his...

'I did not know last night. I did not have a care for...your innocence.' He stood only one more pace away from her now.

Then his words sank through the haze of arousal and she understood what he was asking her.

'I am well,' she said. 'Very well.'

He crossed that last step and took her in his arms. His mouth possessed hers as she'd hoped he would and she lost herself in the sensations of being held by him, surrounded by his strength, his heat, his desire. Only the crinkling sound of the letter tucked inside her gown as they embraced broke into the anticipation. Rob released her as he heard it, too.

'What is that?' he asked, watching as she withdrew it from her gown. 'You found something?'

She wished she'd never seen it. In spite of her body's immediate reaction to him, she wished she could have remained blissfully ignorant of her mother's attempt and Rob's lack of action. Lilidh held it out to him and he took it.

Rob unfolded the parchment and was surprised to find his name at the beginning of it. Short— only one sentence—it took him no time to read it. The signature surprised him even more.

'What is this?' he asked, disappointed that she'd backed away from him as he'd read it. 'Where did you find it?' He'd never seen it before, yet it seemed to have been written months ago.

'In the box,' she said, pointing at it. 'It was wrapped in another letter.'

'I have never seen this before, Lilidh,' he explained, handing it back to her. 'I give you my word.'

He could see her trying to decide if she should believe him or not. Again, noises in the corridor, whether the guards were leaving or others arriving, he knew not. Either one was unacceptable since the walls were not a barrier to words spoken.

'Will you walk with me?' he asked her.

They could speak freely on the battlements. He could read nothing on her face, but at her nod, he found her cloak and put it around her. Lifting the latch and nodding at the guards, he escorted her up the stairs, moving slowly and allowing her time to climb at her own pace. In what seemed now to be their custom, they silently walked the perimeter before stopping before the ruined tower.

But now, when there were so many matters to discuss, he waited on her.

'Had my mother written to you before?' she asked, her gaze intent on his face as she waited for his answer. He gave her the truth.

'Never. And I never received that letter.'

'It was in your father's documents, in a small package filled with other personal letters from my father.'

He shook his head. He'd never seen it until she just handed it to him. So, his father kept it from him. Did he think Rob would do something to interfere with the marriage? The letter was dated months—nigh to a year—ago, but just as things began to fall apart between the Mathesons and the MacLeries. A precipitous time for both the clan and for his father.

'Why would your mother send something like that? And send it to me?'

'I know not,' she said with a shrug. 'We never spoke of you after—after you left. Oh, once when the idea of a match to Iain was raised, she asked if things were truly irreconcilable between us.'

'Did she oppose the match?' he asked, walking around her. He did not like her exposed to the winds or possible dangers here on the battlements now.

'No. She spoke in favour of it after meeting Iain. He was older, but was a kind man to me.'

Hearing her speak of her husband, dead or not, twisted his gut. It mattered not that the man had not claimed her—he'd married her, something Rob had not done and could not do. 'So, my father kept this from me?'

'If you never received it, then I think that's the only plausible explanation.'

She smiled then and he felt a great weight lifted off him in that moment. Though the existence of this letter troubled him for other reasons, she could not give him the answers he needed about it.

Lilidh began to walk then, but he grabbed her hand and pulled her back, into his arms. They had something else to discuss before returning to his chambers. Something that would tell him about what she was thinking when it came to what had already happened between them and if anything further would.

But first he pushed the hood of the cloak back and tangled his hands in her glorious hair. Easing her towards him, he tilted down and touched his mouth to hers. She sighed at the contact and he breathed it in. Her lips opened to him and he sought to possess her mouth. She was ravenous in returning the kisses, giving as good as she got, until they broke away, breathless and panting.

'Why did you not tell me the truth?' he asked, kissing his way down her chin to her neck. 'How? How were you still untouched?' Rob paused and met her gaze. Pain lay there. Embarrassment. Humiliation. Shame. Then she turned her gaze away.

'Iain did not wish to,' Lilidh began to explain, but her voice shook and her lips trembled. 'I displeased him.'

'Did he tell you that?' he asked, lifting her chin so he could see her eyes. 'What did he say?'

She pulled free of him then, turning around, taking a step away and then facing him, as though arguing this through in her head and changing her mind with every thought. He grabbed her shoulders to stop her.

'Just tell me what he said to you.'

'He said nothing. Not a word. He just never touched me. He would come to our bed and sleep and leave in the morning. No matter if I was willing, if I offered...' She gasped, then looked horrified at what she'd admitted to him. Then she said something that made his blood boil and the urge to kill rise in his veins. 'My father said I should not expect him to...because of my...injury.'

'Lilidh, listen to me,' he said softly, easing his grip on her, but drawing her closer. 'I was a fool to say such things to you. Iain was a fool. Your—'

He stopped himself before revealing exactly what role her father had played in these matters. Clearly, Connor had overstepped, but Lilidh adored him and would be further devastated to discover his role in these private and humiliating débâcles. Rob would not be the one to ruin that for her after he'd ruined her life already.

If there was one thing he could do for her before sending her back to her family, it would be to let her know that she was not unwanted or unlovable. Her injury was no worse and better even than many battle injuries he'd seen. The healer never said it would change her life in any way, except for the pain that she would have to endure. So, why did her father use it against her as much as he had?

She shivered under his hands and Rob knew he should return her to the warmth before the good of walking was undone.

'Come,' he said, turning her around towards the doorway. 'Let us—'

It happened so fast, he had no time to react or resist.

Lilidh screamed, pushing him away and twisting her body. He felt the piercing, burning pain, but not the weapon or the enemy. Had Lilidh struck him? The force of it threw him against the wall of the tower and his head hit the stones.

Everything began to swirl around him, the dark, the light, Lilidh, screams, yelling until he could do nothing but follow the darkness down.

The last thing he did was to grab hold of her cloak.

'She is mine,' he called out.

Then…darkness.

Chapter Seventeen

Lilidh saw it only at the last moment. Too late to keep him from harm. She'd pushed Rob as the bolt whooshed towards them, but not hard or far enough. But the impact took him the rest of the way down and his head hit the wall.

She screamed for the guards, screamed out his name and then tried to get to him from where she'd fallen. Of all the times for her leg to fail her! Then he grabbed her cloak with his bloody hand. His men reached them then, pulling her to her feet and trying to drag her away from him.

'She is mine,' Rob rasped out. Then, horribly, he lost consciousness and his hold on her.

Tomas took charge then, calling out orders to this one and that, and soon she found herself carried over someone's shoulder down to Rob's chambers. Rob was half-carried, half-dragged in and placed on the smaller bed that was more easily approached. When she went to try to see to his wound, wherever it was, another guard pulled her away with an order to remain sitting.

With another bulky man standing between her and Rob, she could see nothing. Several servants arrived, including Beathas, to whom she called out. Everyone ignored her except the guard Ranald, who blocked her from rising from the chair. Tugging her cloak off, she waited for some sign that he was not dead.

Who had done this? Were they aiming at Rob or at her? Who would have known they would be up on the battlements, or had this been a random attack, one foreshadowing her father's arrival? She thought on the path of the bolt and where they would have been if she'd not reacted at the last moment. Who was their target?

'It came from the north forest, Tomas.' She said it loudly enough to be heard over the cacophony of voices and orders echoing in the chamber. 'Search the north.'

Then, a terrible thing happened—the door opened and a tearful, sobbing Lady Tyra came running in, with several maids following. Spar-

ing a fleeting glance in her direction, Tyra ran to
Rob's side—and no one stopped her. She was his
betrothed, after all, with more standing here than
Lilidh had. And, as the future lady here, respect
paid to her now would be a well-spent thing.

'Rob! Rob! Speak to me,' she cried out, falling
to her knees at his side. 'Beathas, where was he
struck?'

Clearly she'd been abed when the news arrived
to her, for she wore only a shift with a bed robe
over it. Her hair flowed around her like a fiery
curtain as she moved, the flames in the hearth
reflecting off the red and gold hues in her hair.

Before Beathas or anyone could answer her, a
loud curse rent the chamber. 'Dear God, get off
me!'

Lilidh pushed up from the seat, only to be
held there. Rob was alive! From the complaining and cursing, he was more angry than hurt at
this point. She peeked around Ranald's girth and
saw him climbing up from the bed. He said something more quietly to Tyra, who left the chamber
more quietly than she'd entered.

No matter how much she'd like to ascribe good
intentions to the lady's actions—as Rob's be-

trothed she should—something about Tyra made Lilidh suspicious. Though her brother Symon was odious and dangerous, Tyra reminded Lilidh of a serpent, hiding in the tall grass, waiting to strike. Chills tore through her as the lady walked past her to leave the chamber. The dead blue eyes that stared at her in that moment frightened her more than Symon had or could.

Ranald moved aside—Rob's command to do so was shouted loudly enough for her to hear—and then she could finally see him. Other than the blood on his hand—well, and the bolt still sticking out of his side—he seemed more angry than hurt.

'Rob,' she said, 'you are hurt.' Beathas reached for him, but he waved her off.

'I should be dead,' he replied and everyone in the chamber went silent. 'If you had not pushed me, I would be dead.'

She could not respond then, so many emotions racing through her mind and heart. He would have died. Tears burned her eyes and throat then, but she refused to let them fall. Whatever was between them was not for others to see.

'I but tripped,' she said, trying to sound calm and uncaring.

He stared at her as he allowed Tomas and Beathas to remove his leather jacket and shirt to find the head of the bolt. She dared not look away, even when Beathas grabbed it and pulled it free of his flesh. She may have gasped. She may have startled. She did not look away.

Tomas left Rob and came to her side then, forcing her attentions to him. 'Lady, you saw it come from the north?' he asked, crouching down to speak to her quietly.

'Aye, Tomas. When I glanced up, I saw it against the moon in that last second. From the north.'

'Look at this, Ranald. Tomas,' Rob said. 'The markings on this.' Rob held the bloodied bolt out to them. 'I have seen this man's work before.'

She waited to learn more, but he sent the men off with whispered orders as he allowed Beathas to bandage the wound. Then he dismissed the healer and the last of the servants and Lilidh knew he would leave, too.

'Perhaps they were aiming for me?' she said, trying to lighten the horrible tension within her.

He could have died—should have, if the shooter's aim had been better or if she had not intervened.

'I doubt it, Lilidh,' he said, walking to her as he pulled a new shirt on and tied the laces. Grabbing his jacket, he faced her. 'The man who made that bolt is from Lairig Dubh.'

She lost her footing and fell to the chair, shaking her head as she landed. 'That is not possible, Rob. They would not—'

'Not what, Lilidh? Try to kill me and head off any meaningful resistance on their arrival? Send some watchers with orders to take a shot if they got the opportunity? Tell me, since you know your father's methods so well, would he not order such a thing?'

His voice was calm, almost too calm, as he made his accusation and it frightened her. But something kept rolling over and over in her mind. 'If I had not pushed you out of the way, that bolt would have hit me.'

He blinked then and ran his hands through his hair as he did when something bothered or bewildered him. Staring up at the ceiling as though he could see through the roof to the battlements, he stood silent for several seconds, thinking about her words. When he turned back to face her, Rob's expression was more puzzled than before.

'Who then, Lilidh? Who would try to kill you with a bolt from your clan's fletcher?'

It did not take much thinking to come up with the name of someone who would benefit from either death—Symon.

'Who else?' she asked. Rob did not look as though he wanted to believe it.

'How would he get that?' he asked. Before she could suggest a way, he answered himself. 'From your travelling party. From those guarding and escorting you.'

'After he killed them,' she added. 'If we had not moved, that could have killed both of us.'

Their deaths together would have taken care of so many problems. Symon could have claimed that since a MacLerie bolt killed them both, the Mathesons were not responsible for her death. Since every indication had been made that they were willing to negotiate to a peaceful conclusion, the MacLerie's bolt was the act of war. And Rob's death would clear the way for Symon to be laird.

Dastardly planning, but cunning.

'I am surprised you pushed me away while you still suspected me of receiving that letter from your mother and denying it.'

Lilidh shook her head. She'd forgotten what they'd been discussing when the bolt flew towards them. And there was no way she could allow the man she loved to remain in harm's way.

The gravity of that realisation and the closeness to death for both of them hit her hard then. The tears flowed then, freely, as she ran the couple of paces between them and launched herself into his arms. Unable to be gentle, she held him close and sobbed. He could have died.

He would have died.

Rob held her and let her sob out the fear that he saw take hold of her. Not unlike the nervousness that could happen after a battle was done and the danger gone, he'd seen it taking control of her as they talked about who could be responsible for this attack. Smoothing back her hair and ignoring the burning pain in his side, he held her and let her calm down before trying to do anything else.

She had saved his life. He had no doubt of it. Though he did have misgivings over her being the target, she was correct that, had it hit them directly, there was little chance they would have survived. Her death alone would cause the Mathesons more trouble, but their deaths together by a MacLerie bolt could have ended this encounter—not happily for either clan, but without other lives being lost. His death? Well, the case could be made to Connor that retribution had been paid for Rob's kidnapping of Lilidh and, with her safe return, the situation would have ended.

Lilidh quieted in his arms, so he eased himself away from her and lifted her face to his. The worry and fear in her eyes had not lessened, but the tears had.

'I must go now,' he said, waiting for her to relinquish her grasp on him. 'I will return, Lilidh.'

'Have a care, Rob,' she whispered.

He kissed her and would have kept kissing her had she not stepped back from him. He walked to the door and lifted the latch. Before leaving, he warned her, 'Speak to no one about what happened. Do not share our suspicions with anyone, Lilidh.'

At her nod, he left, pausing in the corridor to catch his breath. He'd faced death or danger many times before in his life, fighting with Connor or lately in skirmishes with his clan, but never had he faced it in his own home. Pressing on the bandage and tightening the buckles of his jacket to keep the pressure on his side, he made his way down to the yard where his men waited on his orders.

Several hours passed as his men searched the nearby forest for any indication that a MacLerie force or spies had arrived on his lands. Finding none, he secured the gates and set more soldiers to watch from along the walls and the gates. Dougal, along with Symon, had been sent out earlier along with others to patrol the village and farms and would not return until the morrow.

Had Symon been behind this attack? Dougal would never have let him return without sending word to Rob, so he doubted he had sent the bolt flying. But that did not mean he did not arrange for it to be done.

He had been walking the battlements each night since the day Lilidh had been brought here—at first alone and then more recently with her. Anyone who lived in the keep would have seen them there. Before going inside, he examined the battlements from the ground and then from the wall that encircled the keep and yard.

If he was right, a MacLerie did not shoot the bolt at all.

Deciding to prove or disprove his suspicion before sharing it with Tomas or Dougal, Rob called for a bow from one of the guards, nocked an arrow and took aim at the battlements. Waiting until the guards moved out of his range, he then let the arrow fly. It hit nearly the same spot where he'd stood earlier.

A MacLerie had not shot at him—a Matheson had.

Worse, the shot had been taken from on top of his own walls.

Rob returned the bow without saying a word to anyone. They had a traitor in their midst. He called the commanders of those who guarded the walls together and asked about who had been on duty earlier. By the time he discovered who it was, he also learned that the man had gone out to search the forest and not returned.

No one could say they knew the man. He'd arrived in the last days, when the farmers and villagers had, spoken to few and served on the wall this night for the first time. Since, by Rob's own orders, all able-bodied men would work where and as they could to help protect the keep, he had no doubt that this man slipped in with the others and waited to carry out his purpose. And then he left, possibly before even knowing if he'd been successful in his attempt.

He doubled the number of guards on the wall and ordered them repositioned, so that every man would be in view of others and no hiding places were possible. Then Rob ordered the entire keep searched for any man who could not be vouched for by two others. Returning to his chambers, he understood that there was little chance of finding an accomplice now.

And more than that bothered him. A traitor might be known to all of them and be hiding in plain sight of all of them. Worse, would the first one leave without knowing if he'd been successful unless there was someone else waiting to try again? Or was his true intention not to kill Rob and Lilidh, but only scare them?

Rob sent word to all the elders that they would meet on the morrow and then he climbed the stair to his chambers. Between the wound, hit-

ting his head and then spending hours searching in the forest and the keep, exhaustion built
within him. A few hours' rest and he would face
all the final tasks needed before the MacLeries
arrived. And he had no doubt that their arrival
would come soon.

Chapter Eighteen

The fire was banked and the room silent when he opened the door. Moving as quietly as he could across the unfamiliar chamber, he found his way to the bed and began to undress. Lilidh lay unmoving, on the side she favoured, facing the hearth.

The wound stung now in spite of the bandage and that it had stopped bleeding some time ago. The metal bolt had luckily skidded across his rib and not penetrated deeply, so he would face mostly this nuisance pain. It was not large enough to cause him to worry about long-lasting effects. He pulled his shirt over his head, hissing against the sudden pull. Dropping his plaid, he realised he'd not barred the door, or put his sword and dagger by the bed.

Rob reached the door and lifted the wooden

bar into place. Other nights, he'd not felt the need to use it, but now, well, now was different. He reached for his sword and dagger, left in his belt and scabbard, when she spoke.

'Do you need those with the door barred?' she asked.

He watched as she slipped from the bed and walked across the chamber, her limp much less pronounced than it had been just days ago. The shift she wore hid few of her curves as she passed by the hearth and in front of a lantern left lit there.

'Yes. Tonight I take no chances,' he replied, pulling both blades free of their scabbards and walking to the bedside. Positioning them where he could reach them quickly, the sword on the floor, the dagger beneath the mattress, he turned back to her.

'Do you have a lump on your head from your fall?' she asked. 'You seemed to wake quickly enough, but I do not think Beathas had time to thoroughly examine the rest of you.'

He must be losing his mind or be so exhausted that he heard something very suggestive in the tone of her voice. When she walked towards him and began touching the bandage, his body reacted on its own to her soft probing caresses. Rob took in and let out a breath before answering.

'I think your father was correct about one thing—I have a hard head.'

'Let me check. I have some experience with injuries like this,' she said. Pointing to the chair, she directed him to sit as she moved behind him. He sat down, his cock hard and expectant, but she either took no notice or said nothing on purpose.

Her fingers gently moved over his scalp, sliding through his hair, moving over the bones and checking the skin as she did. And the result of her stroking was to arouse him even more. The exhaustion that had sent him to seek his rest vanished under her touch. Now she stood in front of him, her breasts only inches away from his face, leaving him with the growing urge to touch them, to taste her.

'You have a bump,' she said. 'Here.' She touched a spot that was sensitive, but another part of him reacted.

When she leaned down and touched her mouth where her fingers had been, his body shook. But, after the revelations of last night and the shocks of this one, he would not touch her until she gave him permission to do so. If it killed him, he would not touch her first. Her soft strokes stopped then and he waited for one...two...three seconds before lifting his head to look at her face.

'I thought I'd lost you tonight, Rob.' Her voice whispered over him, gently moving the air between their faces. 'I know that we will separate when this ends, but I do not want you to die. Not for me and not because of me.'

'I will find a way through this, Lilidh. Fear not,' he said, reaching up to touch her face.

'Will you?' she asked. She lowered her head down until their mouths nearly touched and stopped. Her breath was hot against his face. 'Until then, will you be mine?'

Of all the things he thought she'd say or want, that was not one of them. He expected her to ask him to leave her alone, not to—to want him.

'If you'll have me?'

'I will,' she said, just before placing her lips on his in a kiss that made his heart weep. Afraid to move for fear she would stop, he remained there, under her touch, under her mouth, letting her lead him in this new dance of theirs.

She kissed his mouth lightly, feathering one after the another, along his chin and on to his neck. Then when he was fighting to keep his hands off her, she returned to his mouth and touched her tongue to his lips. He opened to her and tasted her as she dipped into his mouth, seeking his tongue. Her hair fell around them, moving each time she did, skimming their skin with its silky length. Rob twisted it around his hand and held it.

The moment when he lost control was when Lilidh reached down and touched his erection. Wrapping her soft fingers around him, she began to caress and stroke and his body burned hotter with each moment of contact. He reached out to touch her, drawing patterns on her belly.

'Take it off,' he said, tugging on the shift she wore.

'No, Rob.' She worried her lower lip with her teeth and began to step away.

'Take it off, Lilidh. I would see all of you. Now.'

Her body shivered when he spoke, but then fear settled in her gaze and he thought she would refuse him. The fear of someone seeing her leg held her back from enjoying the physical side of marriage. Bold in every other way, she let this control her and so she let her father use it to control her life.

It ended now.

Rob slid his fingers under the edge of the fabric and he pulled her to stand between his legs with it. He had ignored, or avoided, touching the injured skin when he'd loved her last night, but he would not this night. He closed his hand and used the back of it to slide along her leg, over her knee and towards the worst of the damage.

She leaned away the slightest bit, as though thinking about moving out of his grasp, but then she stopped. He could not even hear her breathing now. His hand reached the first area of scarred skin, the surface marbled with grooves. Her hand touched his, but he moved it away and went back to exploring her body.

He lifted the shift and she pulled it off over her head, tossing it aside and leaving herself completely exposed to him.

God, she was a beauty!

And she was his now.

He let go of his restraint and leaned towards her, his mouth touching and tasting her. He did not avoid the damaged skin or muscle, but instead began there, kissing and stroking it as he did every other place he could reach. Tempted to stand, he remained seated, for it gave him the perfect access to her. When he felt Lilidh begin to tremble, he slid his hands between her legs.

The puzzled look on her face told him she had no idea of how to seek pleasure in this position. Her body was ready enough that he would not hurt her by entering her this way.

'Ride me, Lilidh,' he said, guiding her forwards until she stood straddling his legs with his arousal waiting below her. A smile lit up her features for a moment when she understood, but was quickly replaced by the look of determination he knew well. Then, with his hands on her hips, he supported her as she tilted down and took him inside her.

The groan could have been his or hers, he knew and cared not, the exquisite torment of her sheathing him replacing any thoughts. Like sliding into a glove made for him, he inched upwards slowly, claiming her once more. Once seated completely within her, he waited as she became accustomed to his length.

'Put your hands on my shoulders,' he instructed. Now the true pleasure could begin.

Lilidh did as he said and held on to his shoulders. Running her hands on the muscles, she enjoyed the strength she felt. Each time she caressed him, his hard flesh inside of her would shudder. Then her body would answer by tightening around him. Such a wondrous thing! She tried not to tense up when his hands moved to her thighs and one rested on the scarred skin where the horse's hoof had torn into her leg.

'Worry not, love,' he whispered as though he could read her thoughts and fears. 'Move like this.' His body arched beneath her, driving him further inside and making her gasp. She felt every inch of him there.

With her feet on the floor and her hands on his shoulders, she could push her body along his thighs and control his depth and, as her body blossomed with heat during each movement, the pleasure. She let her head fall back as she concentrated on how to move. Then, at some point, she forgot it all and just moved.

His mouth on her breasts intensified the throbbing between her legs. When he sucked on the

sensitive nipple of one, she moaned out in pleasure. He thrust his hips, aiding in her movements
until she could only feel...everything! Her skin
burned, her body ached and needed more, more
of him, more friction inside, more...

When Rob moved to torture the other nipple,
cupping his hands under her breasts and flick-
ing his thumbs across the tightened tips, it was
like there was a rope connecting all the aroused
places inside of her to every other place in her
body. His thumb teased the tip and she felt the
pull of it throughout her. When he took the nipple inside between his teeth, she screamed out.
Her body trembled and shook, the tension building and burning through her.

He laughed against her skin and she shuddered.

The touch of his hand, sliding down over her
and searching between her legs, surprised her. He
put his other hand behind her head and pulled her
mouth to his. Then, he tormented her, his tongue
deep in her mouth while his fingers searched and
teased. The feel of him inside and out, moving
deeper and faster, excited her even more. But the
moment when he found some small spot with his

finger and touched it, caressing it and pressing against it, tore all reason from her.

Her body careened out of control and she moaned against his mouth as the pleasure peaked and exploded in her. Her muscles clenched around his flesh until she felt his release within her. Rob became relentless then, until Lilidh could not do a thing. How many times had she cried his name? How many times had her body reached that peak and fallen over? She knew not.

Exhausted, she fell against him and felt his arms surround her, holding her close as his heart and breathing returned to its normal pace. Hers? Hers might have stopped altogether for all she knew. Minutes passed but she could not move away from him. Her legs would not obey her commands and the rest of her was held captive by the blissful lethargy that filled her blood now.

Some time later, the chill air in the chamber on her still-sweaty skin reminded her of her nakedness and her position on his legs. He gradually eased out of her and she felt empty again. Embarrassed now by her lack of reserve, she thought about what she should say to him.

What did a well-born, well-raised noblewoman say to her lover after such a display of unashamed lust?

He kissed the top of her head and then rubbed her back in a soothing motion. 'Did that hurt?' he asked quietly.

'No,' she said, lifting herself off his chest and meeting his gaze. 'Not my leg.'

'Was it too much too soon after...?' His eyes searched her face. 'After the first time.'

She stroked his face and kissed him. 'No. It was...wondrous.' That was the only word she could think of.

'Yes,' he said, kissing her back. 'Wondrous.'

'And now?' she finally asked, uncertain about what to do next.

'Now, I carry you to that bed and we get under the warm covers,' he said. 'It is getting cold in here.'

Rob rose to his feet without moving her and then lifted her into his arms. He laughed as he tossed her on the bed and pulled the covers down. Soon they were lying in his bed with his arms around her. At first, touching skin to skin seemed very strange, but his warmth and the easy way he touched her soothed any misgivings she might have.

Lilidh did not know when she fell into sleep's grasp, but she knew when she awoke. Lying on her side, his hand caressed her breast, tickling and teasing it gently. His mouth kissed her ear and his breath sent shivers of heat through her body. When her body arched against him, he slipped his hand further down.

He hardened between their bodies as he stroked her. Without a word, he eased her hips back towards him and slid between her thighs. This time he built the need within her slowly and quietly until she shattered under his touch and his possession.

Lilidh lost count of the times and the ways in which they joined through that night, but when dawn's light shone through the windows of his bedchamber she knew one thing.

Though she might leave here and return to Lairig Dubh, her heart would always remain with

Rob. For in that night filled with pleasure and passion, he'd made her feel whole again for the first time since her body had been torn apart.

Chapter Nineteen

The next two days passed by quickly for Rob—
he barely stopped in one place for more than a
few minutes. Tasks awaited him around every
corner.

The meeting with the elders went well. Though
they would not relent and release Lilidh as he
wanted them to do, he did gain their support
for him to handle the coming negotiations with
the MacLeries. Even Murtagh begrudgingly accepted his plan to get out of this peacefully.

Symon seemed genuinely stunned by news of
the attack when he returned to Keppoch Keep
with Dougal and the others and Rob could discover no link between Symon and the stranger.
Still, with his suspicions growing, Rob thought it
best to set some watchers on Symon over the next
few days. Choosing a few trustworthy men, he

ordered them to keep watch over what his cousin did and with whom he met.

One decision he'd made was that he would not sign the official betrothal contract with Tyra. No matter what breach existed between his line and Symon's, marriage to Tyra would not heal it. The thought of marrying once Lilidh left his life for good held little appeal to him.

Tensions ran high as the days passed with the pending arrival of the MacLeries and possibly war at their gates. Fights broke out among some of the farmers and warriors. Supplies went missing.

His only respite was with Lilidh.

After that night, she held nothing back from him. Never seemed uncomfortable with him, in bed or out. They would lose themselves in their growing passion as soon as one touched the other and hours passed spent wrapped around each other in his bed.

He began to take his evening meal with her in his chambers so they could discuss his plans to deal with her family...and his. She'd organised all the letters between her father and his and now there seemed a pattern to them. Though he remembered nothing that could have caused it, other than his own immaturity, clearly some deep, personal insult had happened between his father and Connor.

Had youthful stupidity really caused the rift between them? And how could he, or could he, solve this puzzle before Connor arrived?

Just before full dark, two nights later, the MacLeries arrived on his land and set up camp. He stopped counting the fires of the encampment when he reached two score. They approached no further and made no attempt to send word or greeting to him, but their appearance and numbers terrified those within the walls.

No one slept that night.

Lilidh had stood watching at the window for hours before he coaxed her to bed. Once in his arms, she had become like a wild thing, loving him with a desperation he'd never seen before.

When morning and the call came, she sat with haunted eyes and watched him leave the bed-chamber.

The Beast of the Highlands had come calling at Keppoch Keep—and God help them all.

Rob emptied the hall of everyone and only permitted a few of the elders, Dougal, Symon—now tanist and heir if Rob died or did not produce a son—Tyra and several guards to remain. He gave explicit instructions on what he expected to happen and what he expected of them. Dougal left to give the oath of truce so that the MacLeries could enter under the promise of hospitality.

With the rest seated behind him, Rob stood and waited for them to enter and the real battle to begin. The sounded of their approach echoed ahead of them into the hall. The nervous whispers behind him ceased as they entered and approached.

A huge man led the way in and Rob would have recognised Rurik Erengilsson anywhere. At a half more than six feet tall and still carrying the weight and muscles of his youth, the half-Norse, half-Scottish leader of all MacLerie warriors had lost nothing with age. Rob could feel every bruise the man had ever given him in training and knew him to be a deadly adversary. Rurik stopped and stepped aside as the negotiator walked forwards.

Duncan MacLerie knew how to bargain and would wrestle the best terms in any treaty for the MacLeries. Years spent building a reputation as such, he'd also trained his stepdaughter and they had travelled extensively on the Earl of Douran's business concerns. Rob had learned much from Duncan's tutelage during his time being fostered in Lairig Dubh and facing this man on opposite sides of a dispute did not please him.

Rob waited for Duncan to stand aside so he could greet Connor and take his measure, but when the man did move, a woman stood behind him, arms crossed and fire in her eyes.

'Jocelyn MacCallum, Lady MacLerie, the Countess of Douran,' Duncan said loudly. The gasps behind him let him know that they understood her position. Rob glanced back and motioned to them to rise in respect for the woman in their midst.

'Lady MacLerie,' he said, bowing to her. 'I did not expect you.' Jocelyn walked right up to him and glared at him. Barely reaching his chest, she did not let her lack of height stop her from trying to intimidate him.

'You may have remembered your manners, *Laird* Matheson, but clearly you have lost your wits,' she said before delivering a stinging slap to his face.

Both Rurik and Duncan began to move in his direction, and hers, but he waved them off. Bowing once more to her, Rob understood the fear that lay deep in her eyes. She reacted as a mother whose bairn was in danger. He could and would excuse it, once. When she opened her mouth to speak, he decided he needed to take control over this and find out when Connor would arrive.

'Lady MacLerie, you are overwrought from your journey and your worries about your daughter. I would remind you she is still in my custody.'

'If you have harmed her—' she began. Duncan furiously whispered her name and Rurik sighed and rolled his eyes, but she ignored them. 'There is nothing and no one that will stop me from finding you, Rob Matheson, and making you regret what you've done.'

'Laird Matheson,' Duncan said in a calm voice. It felt very strange indeed to be called such by him. 'Is it possible to allow Lady MacLerie to see to Lady MacGregor?'

'Tomas,' Rob called out without taking his gaze off Jocelyn. 'Escort Lady MacLerie to see her daughter.'

Since he had fully expected this situation, he'd already given Tomas orders about the length of the visit and that, under no circumstances, should he leave them alone. Jocelyn took a step towards the other doorway in the hall, but Tomas pointed towards the stairs. She'd expected Lilidh to be in their dungeon?

'She is being held in my chambers,' he explained. The news did not go over well with any of them. Rob waited for Jocelyn to leave before asking the question he wanted answered most.

'When does Connor arrive?' he asked Duncan.

The two MacLeries exchanged glances and then Duncan answered, 'We represent the laird here. We negotiate in good faith in his name.'

Rob's temper flared at the insult. Connor had sent his men to deal with him and sort out the problem. He did not come himself. Once more, Rob was not worthy of the time or effort. Duncan must have seen his reaction in spite of his attempts to control it and keep his expression blank. The man was an expert in understanding people so it was probably as clear as if Rob had shouted it aloud.

'Laird.' Tyra's voice broke into the conversation. He had not heard her approach and had forgotten to make her and the others known to the MacLeries. 'May I offer some food and drink to our guests while you wait for Lady MacLerie's return?'

Rob nodded. Tyra motioned Duncan and Rurik forwards to the table that had been prepared for just this. When they were seated, Rob introduced each of his family and counsellors.

Once they had had a chance to partake, he dismissed everyone but Dougal, Symon and the elders.

'I would speak plainly, Laird,' Duncan began. 'If you release the lady now, all of this is done. Connor will take no offence and you can go on your way.'

'No offence?' Symon asked. Rob glared at him, but it did not stop him. 'We are offended that the laird himself did not answer our demands in person.'

'The earl has many pressing duties, sir,' Duncan replied in a low, respectful tone. 'Since this is a personal issue and one of some delicacy, he thought it best—'

'To treat the Mathesons as he was always treated us—not important enough to matter.' Symon stood then. 'The MacKenzies have offered to back us in this, MacLerie. They are just as powerful as you and their friendship has been offered and accepted.'

Unfortunately, the elders agreed with Symon in this and Rob felt himself losing control of the situation. He'd not accepted the MacKenzie's offer yet. Glancing at each of them, it was clear that someone had. He felt as though he was fighting with one hand tied to his foot and a blindfold over his eyes.

And Duncan missed none of this. The shrewd negotiator was a watcher first—he studied his opponents before beginning his work. Before giving him more time to determine all of their weaknesses, Rob stood.

'I will send Lady MacLerie to you, Duncan. We will begin our discussions when Connor arrives.'

'He is not coming, Rob,' Duncan said quietly. 'You know him—that's not how he handles things.'

'Surely his daughter's safety is worth his time.'

'Is she in danger?' Duncan asked.

Rurik looked bothered when Duncan asked his question and Rob knew that was not a good sign. Bothered was one step away from angry and anger was dangerous in a man like Rurik. Rob had seen Rurik *angry* and did want to unleash that here in his hall. Or on his lands. Or on his clan, no matter how much they frustrated him.

'You may go now. I will send Lady MacLerie to you in the yard,' he repeated. He needed to get them out of the hall and discover what behind-his-back arrangements were going on with the damned MacKenzies. Although Rurik looked ready to take his head, Duncan nodded and stood.

'May we return later this day and speak again, Laird Matheson?' he asked, his tone respectful and even, not meant to inflame, but to engender reasonableness.

'Laird?'

Rob turned when Symon used the title, for he never had before, not in private and not in public. 'We will speak in private, Symon.' He gave a slight shake to his head to tell Symon this was not the time.

'Until later, then,' Duncan said as they turned to leave.

Rob watched until they left, escorted out by Dougal, and then he climbed the stairs to seek out Jocelyn in his chambers. When he arrived, he walked quietly down the hall, signalling to Tomas who stood at the door not to announce his presence. Standing silently beyond their sight, he listened as mother and daughter spoke within.

'I told you, Mother. I am well.'

'Those bruises say otherwise, Lilidh,' Jocelyn chided.

'Would you have expected me to give up without a fight? They killed my guards, almost killed my maid.'

'Isla?' Jocelyn asked.

'Is recovering downstairs, Lady MacLerie,' he said, walking in then.

They sat side by side on a long bench before one

of the windows. Mother and daughter, holding hands, and leaning on each other as they talked. What had Lilidh told her about him? About them? Her gaze caught his as he walked towards them and it was unreadable. Did Jocelyn know?

'Rob, I beg your pardon for slapping you,' Jocelyn said, standing and letting go of Lilidh's hand. 'I beg you not to hold Lilidh accountable for my—'

'Bad behaviour?' he asked.

'She hit you?' Lilidh asked, as she stepped over closer and looked at his face.

'Like daughter, like mother,' he said

'I have never struck you,' Lilidh argued.

'You tried, when you were brought here.' Rob realised that Jocelyn was watching their actions closely—too closely. Did they wear their intimacy like a garment so that others could see it?

'Your men wait for you in the yard, Lady MacLerie.' Rob turned and motioned to the door. 'Tomas will escort you down to them.'

Though she looked as if she wanted to fight with him, Jocelyn hugged and kissed Lilidh farewell and left with Tomas. When they'd gone, he closed the door, not certain of his welcome in his own chambers.

She'd been crying, that much he could see. But had it done her any good to see her mother for such a brief time?

'I am surprised your father allowed her to journey here,' he said. Though…

'I doubt that my mother gave him a choice in the matter. I could not believe my eyes when Tomas opened the door and she stood there. I expected you to return, but never did I think I would see her.'

'And?' Rob asked.

'I have not seen her since I married Iain, Rob.'

Jocelyn had no idea of the state of Lilidh's marriage. Glancing past her, he realised the bed was yet unmade. Had Jocelyn noticed and understood?

'She asked. I told her the truth—that I've been sharing your bed.'

Lilidh was looking at the bed, too. Sadness tinged her words, yet her eyes did not show it. Rob slid his fingers around hers, entwining them together and kissing her hand.

'Regrets now?' he asked. It would not surprise

him if she was having them, especially now since her mother knew.

Their time-out-of-time was over now. Duty and family called both of them. The nights of acting as if they were meant to be together was done. The acts committed in this bed would now become memories and be the only part of her left to him when she departed here.

'Nay, no regrets, Rob.'

But she let his hand drop and then went to straighten the bedcovers without saying more. He watched her perform such a menial, everyday task and the longing nearly took him down as the bolt had.

'I will be meeting with your cousins later. Do you have any greetings to send them? Or have you already told your mother?'

'No. You do what you must and they will do that as well,' she said softly.

'Lilidh—' He stopped because he just did not know what he could say.

He could not promise to keep her—his clan depended on giving her back in order to survive. He could not offer her his love—for she and he would both be expected to marry elsewhere. He could not tell her the truth—for it would tear her world and her heart apart.

'Just go and do what you must, Rob.'

He turned to go, but he did want to hear her opinion on one matter before he did.

'Why do you think your father did not come to get you, Lilidh? Why is he not here, beating down my doors to get to you?'

She shook her head and looked over at him. 'Because a daughter is not a reason to go to war. Because one person in a battle is expendable,' she offered. The haunted expression was back in her eyes when she faced him. 'I know you expected him to answer your challenge, but it's truly better if only Duncan and Rurik are here instead.'

Thinking back on the way Connor handled matters during Rob's time at Lairig Dubh made him realise a pattern he'd not seen before or had forgotten since—Connor went only after other measures failed to resolve a conflict. When Connor went....

'Because if the *Beast* comes, you will die,' she finished. 'You will all die.'

Then they were in deeper trouble than he thought they could be! He'd demanded that Connor face him over this, thinking it would scare off the Mathesons from this foolhardy plan to ransom her, to smack at her father's nose. Now he might have brought the destruction to them that he had wanted to avoid.

No matter his personal need to confront Connor over sins of the past and to discover the reason for his actions, bringing him here to Keppoch and facing him publicly was too dangerous to the rest of his kith and kin. The only thing he must accept was that any attempt to keep Lilidh, to claim her as his heart and soul wanted him to do, would be as unacceptable to Connor now as it was four years ago.

There would be one way to know if Connor wished the past to remain buried—if he gave gold in return for Lilidh. If he took that easier path to resolution, it was a way to avoid everything else.

And if Connor offered him gold?

The only thing Rob could do was to take it and send her back. To admit that this time they'd shared was the extraordinary time it had been and to let her move on in her life, hopefully healed of some of the damage he'd done before.

Rob left the chambers then, heading for the elders and Symon. He must convince them to release Lilidh as soon as possible. His reckoning with Connor would have to wait for another time.

Tyra watched the rest of this first meeting from a hidden corner just out of view of the rest. When Symon exploded with his accusation that the MacLerie was marginalising both the Mathesons and their demands, she'd nearly lost control and laughed aloud. Then the look on Rob's face when Symon revealed that a deal had been struck with the MacKenzies without his knowledge was more satisfying than she had ever imagined it would be.

It had been favours and gold well spent to set that part up. Luckily she'd found Brother Donal to be more a man of worldly concerns than godly ones and the deal to forge certain documents had been struck. His return to the abbey at Angus's untimely death had ensured that only his confessor, and that under the holy seal, would ever hear any claims he made.

And the gold spent encouraging one or two of the elders to continue their enthusiastic support of Symon and his opinions was also done well.

None of them would open their mouths or risk exposure as traitors and being named outlaw.

Symon had come to her before this meeting and told her that Rob suspected him of ordering the attack. She hoped she'd kept a concerned expression in her eyes as her brother demonstrated to her once again what kind of fool he was!

So, she'd stoked his anger at being left out of decisions and at Rob's suspicions until Symon was ready to explode. Then she'd watched as he had—revealing more to the MacLeries than Rob knew.

Leaning back against the wall, she waited for the MacLeries to leave the keep before seeking her chambers. Though Rob had dismissed her, Symon would come and apprise her of anything said or ordered. And, in turn, she would push and prod Symon to make certain the hostilities between him and Rob continued.

Tyra made her way back to her chambers and found the small casket in which she kept trinkets and keepsakes hidden. The letter lay on top and she opened the parchment and read it once more. Gavin swore his undying love for her and urged her to remain in her faith of him.

Certainly she knew of his proclivity to sleep with the servants—her spy there revealed that to her—but that did not lessen their love. It was only until she took her place as his wife and then she would see to that much as she had been seeing to things here.

Chapter Twenty

Rob strode into the large chamber that he used as a solar and found them waiting for him. Along with the elders, Symon and Dougal sat stone-faced and silent. Brother Finlay entered just behind him, carrying his usual leather satchel with documents, quills, ink and a sharp knife with which to scrape off old used parchments for reuse. A guard closed the door and Rob looked at each man there.

'Symon mentioned an agreement with the MacKenzies. I know of no such thing,' he began. 'How is that?' Then he crossed his arms and waited for someone to answer his question.

He knew he was being manoeuvred and manipulated, but he did not think Symon intelligent enough to do that. His outburst was a perfect example of how he acted—too fast, too loud and too much. Subtlety was lost on him. Looking around at the others, he tried to decide who could be the one.

'My lord,' Brother Finlay began, 'I found this in your father's papers. Since you were...ahem... involved in some matter, I showed it to Lord Symon.' Involved in the carnal knowledge of a certain lady was what Brother Finlay did not say, but they understood what had caught Rob's attention lately.

If he trusted Symon as a chief should trust his tanist, Rob might have felt differently about that. But Symon's interference and attempts to push him in only one direction broke what trust they might have had at one time.

Rob took the parchment and walked away from the table, reading it. Although it was not a formal treaty, this did make a preliminary proposal and an agreement to proceed with one. It was written by his father's clerk and signed by the laird himself and the marks matched the others of his father's that he'd seen. 'Why was this not among my father's other documents? Among the ones I have in my possession.'

'I know not, my lord,' the cleric answered

with a shrug. 'I found it in one of the trunks that Brother Donal left when he returned to the abbey. I assumed you knew of it, but with all this talk about treaties and war with the MacLeries, I thought it best to bring it to your attention.'

'And when did you bring this to the tanist?' he asked. Symon began to speak, but Rob waved him off.

'Only yesterday, my lord.' Brother Finlay, a large man, wiped at his sweating brow with the sleeve of his brown robe. 'As I said, all this talk...'

'Does anyone in this room have knowledge of a formal treaty with the MacKenzies?' he asked quietly and then he waited to give someone, anyone, a chance to answer. When none did, he continued. 'Has anyone been in contact with the MacKenzie laird or others since my father died?'

'Rob, you know I have spoken to my father's cousins there,' Symon replied. 'My support of that is not unknown.'

He laughed then at Symon's understated and unexpected admission. 'I think we all know of your support to break from the MacLeries.' He stopped smiling and waited. 'Any of you have anything to add?' When they did not, when no one else spoke, Rob leaned on the table with his knuckles and shared his knowledge of Connor's methods with them.

'If we are to get out of this situation that Symon has put us in and if we are to get out well enough to continue negotiating with the MacKenzies as you all seem wont to do, I need to know if there will be any other surprises or disclosures. I asked for gold for Lady MacGregor's return and will negotiate her release under those conditions.'

Symon began to argue, but Rob would not hear it. 'You kidnapped her and brought her here, Symon. Though I did not give the orders for that action, as laird and chief, you act on my behalf. I am responsible for what you've done.' Rob stood up and glared at his cousin. 'It is the way of it, Symon! Now, I ask one last time—have promises of any kind been made to the MacKenzie laird?'

Silence filled the chamber for several moments.

'Very well,' Rob said. 'I will meet with the MacLerie peacemaker and see if he can work out a peace between us.'

Rob stood near the door, signalling that this meeting was done and watched as each one left.

He asked Dougal to remain and then he grabbed Symon's arm.

'Cousin. Did you have something else to say?' Something had flashed in Symon's eyes at his last question, but his cousin had said nothing. He just pulled from his grasp and left.

'That went well, did it not?' Dougal asked with a smirk on his face.

'Symon or the whole discussion?' Rob asked.

Dougal walked over to a table in the corner and poured two cups of ale. After he handed one to Rob, he backed up a pace and asked. 'So, will you really return the lady to her family?'

'Aye.' Rob drank most of the ale in one swallow. When Dougal said nothing more, he turned and faced him. 'I did not bring her here, Dougal.'

'I did not think you had,' he replied. Watching him over the rim of the cup, he said, 'But it's clear to anyone with eyes that you are not unhappy she is here and sharing your bed.'

Though Rob wanted to pummel him for bringing up such a thing, he decided not to protest too much. 'She is, as it turns out, a lonely widow.'

'You insult the lady's honour, Rob,' Dougal said in an angry voice. 'And you seem to forget that we have been friends for many years. I saw you when you returned from Lairig Dubh.' Dougal drank again without taking his gaze off Rob. 'And I spent three days with you when your father told you of her marriage. You are a talkative drunk, in case you did not know it.'

He'd been a ranting lunatic in those days. Dougal probably did remember more of it than he did. His friend had taken him somewhere to suffer through it where no one else could be privy to his pain. Or to any of the truth that caused it.

'It cannot be, Dougal. Connor objected then and he'll object now—especially with the way this began. There is no way that does not threaten this clan.'

'If you say so.' Dougal finished his ale and put the cup down. 'You still suspect Symon's motives.'

'Something does not fit, Dougal. He wanted, he wants, to be chief. He wants this clan to be taken seriously and be allies with the best. Some of his actions just do not make any sense.' Rob thought on the day they'd gone riding across the farmlands and villages. 'His suggestions were well thought out and are good ones. They would improve the way we do many things with our crops. His defensive strategies are the same. You said his ideas were intelligent when you travelled with him the other day.'

'Yet he acts out of turn.'

'Aye. As though like an angry dog that has been poked in the eye by someone with a large stick.' Rob shook his head. 'I put two men on him. Mayhap they will see or hear something to explain it.'

'Laird?' The guard spoke from the doorway. 'The lady asks for permission to visit with her maid.'

'Is it a good idea, Rob? To have her roaming through the keep when the MacLeries are at our gates?'

'She is less trouble when she is kept busy, Dougal. Since there is only one way into that chamber, it is easily guarded.' Rob nodded at the guard. 'She may go there now and stay until I say so.'

The guard went off to relay the order.

'And when her mother asks to see her again?' Dougal asked.

Rob smiled. Lady MacLerie was not difficult to understand. She was here for her daughter and wanted to be with her as much as possible. Would the lady talk her daughter out of his bed if he allowed them to keep company together? Rob shrugged against the inevitable and his friend laughed at him as he left to see to another matter.

Rob called a servant in to ready this chamber for the MacLeries' arrival. It was large and private, a good place to hold their talks. Though there would be food and drink provided, it would not be a shared meal, so Rob went off to the kitchens to eat something more substantial before the negotiations began.

And, if he happened to catch a glimpse of Lilidh as she passed through on her way to Isla, well, that was good too. There would be so few days left to them now and he would take advantage of every hour of them.

Symon left Rob and went to see his sister. So many things did not make sense now. Rob did not reject his ideas as Tyra said he would—not about defence or even about changes to some of the farms. So, as he approached her chamber, he decided that he was not so opposed to some of the things Rob wanted to do.

And he would tell Tyra exactly that.

Walking through the hall and up to the tower that held their chambers, Symon realised that Tyra was beginning to overstep her place. He'd heard about her striking Lilidh MacLerie and leaving a mark. If she'd stayed away from Rob's chambers as he'd ordered, that would not have happened.

He knocked and entered without waiting. She should be waiting on him since he'd told her he would come directly here after meeting with Rob and the elders. Instead of her maids attending her, a man he did not know stood there speaking to her.

'Who are you?' he asked, walking towards them. He'd not seen the man before. 'What business do you have here?'

'Symon, this is Connell from the stables. My horse has thrown a shoe and injured her leg. Connell was bringing me news of what needs to be done.' Tyra ushered the man out as Symon watched. Once the door was closed, he berated her.

'Where are your maids? He should not be here in your chambers without a chaperon of some kind. Servant or not.'

'Aye, you are right, Symon,' Tyra said, nodding her head. 'The maids left but a moment before you arrived. I am surprised you did not pass them in the corridor.' She filled a cup and offered it to him. 'Sit and tell me what happened?' When he sat in one of the chairs, she knelt down before him and sat on her heels, looking up at him.

'He was angry about me speaking in front of the MacLeries,' he began.

'Of course he was! You took the strongest position and defended the clan's honour as he should have done.' She patted his leg and smiled at him. Sometimes he forgot that she had been his biggest supporter after their mother died.

By the time he left her chambers, Symon's anger was stoked again over the demeaning way he was being treated when he should be laird and chief. And if someone needed to make that clear, not only to Rob and his cronies, but also to the high-and-mighty MacLeries, well then, who better than him to do it?

Lilidh left Rob's chambers, following Ranald down the stairs. His bulk filled the stone stairway and, at least, she knew if she stumbled, he would block her fall. Her leg seemed stronger over the last day or so and the time it took to reach the bottom was much less than the last time. She paused once there and looked around, hoping and dreading that she would catch a glimpse of her cousins Duncan and Rurik.

They walked through the empty hall and down the corridor to the chamber where Isla stayed. Opening the door for her, Ranald stepped aside so she could enter and then closed the door behind her. Isla slept—once more or still she knew not—and Lilidh sat down at her side. Only a short time had passed when the door opened next. Expecting Siusan with some chore or to see to Isla, her mother entered.

'Rob let you back in? I am surprised!' she said, rising to greet her mother.

'As am I,' her mother replied, laughing. Then she turned her attentions to the woman on the bed. 'Does she sleep constantly?'

'No, Mother. She wakes and sleeps throughout the day.'

'A better sign than sleeping all the time, I think.' Her mother turned and sat on the other stool facing the bed and Lilidh. 'So, now that we have some privacy, can you tell me what happened?'

'Did Duncan send you on this mission, then? You must bring back information he can use?' she asked, only half in jest.

'I will tell him what you say I can, but nothing you do not wish to share.'

Why did she feel like crying now? She had never cried when attacked or brought here. Only the news of her maid Isla's death and the others killed when she was taken brought her to tears. And when she thought she'd lost Rob. Even as a girl, she did not surrender to tears often. But now? One look at her mother's soft expression of concern and she was lost.

One moment she was thinking about how strong she needed to be and the next one found her wrapped in her mother's comforting embrace, crying out a list of emotions she could not name.

'Easy now, sweetling,' her mother whispered, rocking her to and fro as she held her tightly. 'Worry not, let it out,' she said. And Lilidh did.

It was a short while before she could stop the

tears. Then, a few more minutes before she could speak.

'Just tell me the daft man did not force you,' her mother said, under her breath with more than a hint of hostility in her voice. Her mother did not suffer fools well or easy.

'Oh, no,' Lilidh said, sitting up and wiping her face. 'Never.'

Her mother gave her the strangest look then, as though suddenly realising something or recognising something she'd not seen or known before. 'You still love him?'

'Iain?' she replied, misunderstanding apurpose. 'I did care for him.' She looked away then, not daring to meet her mother's astute gaze.

'He broke your heart and yet you still carry soft feelings for him.' Her mother knew.

'I did not know it until now.'

'Was it wise to go to his bed? I know you are a widow, Lilidh, and some might look the other way at a widow seeking some happiness, but this will only complicate matters.'

'I needed to know, Mother,' she admitted in a whisper. 'That must sound scandalous, but 'tis the truth.'

'And he has not offered for you?' Her mother watched her intently now.

'Father would never accept him. You know that. Not after what he did before and now this.'

'Your father can be quite hard-headed,' she began. Lilidh laughed over her choice of words.

'Rob said the same thing about himself. I am content that I had this chance to see how it could be between us.'

'Content?' her mother asked, smoothing her hair from her face. 'Content?'

Thinking about their time together these last several nights, Lilidh knew she was content with her decision. 'Yes, Mother. Content. Rob is trying to do his best for his clan in this, so there can be nothing more for us than what we have shared.'

'He asked for gold, you know. He demanded gold for your return.'

She shrugged. 'They are not a wealthy clan. We are. It would seem a fair exchange. An honourable way out for both sides, especially since this was not Rob's idea.' As soon as the words left her mouth, she wished she'd not revealed that bit. It would reveal how Rob's position here was precarious and give her cousin more power in the stalemate. If her mother realised the significance of it, she did not show it.

Her mother stood then and paced around the room a few times. Never a good sign, Lilidh waited as her mother gathered the nerve to say what she had to say.

'I would think you would want him skinned alive for what he did to you, Lilidh. Why are you not screaming for his head? Demanding his death? Asking that your father destroy this keep and him?'

Lilidh pondered her mother's words. For a long time after Rob had disavowed her, she had thought of nothing but one or two hundred different ways in which he could die—and all of them terrible. But now? After he'd protected her from harm, shared his own fears with her, and after they'd made enough memories to last the rest of her life without him, she understood the duty they each had to carry out.

'Because I have learned about duty, Mother. As has Rob.' Lilidh stood then and faced her mother. 'Whatever happened between us those years ago, it is over between us. Why bring death and destruction to people who had nothing to do with anything in the past?'

A flicker of something passed over her mother's face just then. Something that resembled guilt. Which reminded Lilidh of a question of her own. 'Why did you write to Rob when I was about to marry Iain?'

'He told you? I would have thought he would keep it a secret since he had not the decency to respond.'

'Mother, he never received your letter. His father did and kept it from him,' she explained. 'But why did you send it? Father made his feelings about Rob and the Mathesons quite clear.'

Her mother shook her head and shrugged. ''Twas a mistaken notion, that is all.'

She would have asked more about that, but they were interrupted when Siusan arrived. They spent most of the afternoon there, speaking to Isla when she would rouse, helping her wash and eat, and chatting quietly when she slept. Siusan and her mother renewed their acquaintance, for apparently Siusan's cousin yet lived in Lairig Dubh and owed some debt to her mother that neither woman would identify, but both accepted.

* * *

A few hours passed before a guard came to escort Lilidh back to Rob's chambers. If her mother had an opinion, which from the fire in her eyes, she did, she never spoke about it. After a farewell hug, her mother followed another guard out. They were walking towards the stairway when Symon approached with his sister. If Lilidh backed a step away, she could not help it—she expected the worst. Ranald motioned for her to come along and she did, but she had a bad feeling about this.

Symon greeted her mother with a respectful bow and then stood at her side as Tyra engaged her in a conversation over some matter. As Lilidh left, Rob, Duncan and the others entered the hall to return to their encampment outside the walls. Before they climbed up the three flights of steps, something happened and the sounds of a scuffle or fight, yelling and cursing echoed up through the stairway.

Though she wanted to go back, Ranald took her by the arms and guided her, with force but not harm, the rest of the way. If he hastened her entrance into the bedchamber, it was without malice, and after warning the guard on duty to be alert, Ranald ran back down the stairs. She called out after she heard the bar drop, but the guard, someone she had not seen before, did not answer her.

Minutes passed like hours as she waited for some explanation and to learn if her mother was safe. Symon had done something, possibly something dangerous, most likely something stupid, which would cause more problems for Rob. She could not figure out if Symon wanted to destroy only Rob or the whole Matheson clan.

She stood by the window, staring out as the fires began to light up the forest outside the walls. Staying back in the shadows, she wondered if this was her last night with Rob. Walking to ease the tightness in her leg, she thought about how she felt about leaving him now. Maybe the talk about him with her mother had forced her to consider it more intensely than the scandalous, superficial reason she'd given her mother.

Regardless, she knew she would hurt deeply after she left him than she had when he left her. Though she'd like to think that this time for them had been only about pleasures of the flesh, her heart knew it had been more. And knew it could be more between them.

Yet he would not admit it or explain the whole of how the chasm had opened between them and their fathers. Oh, Rob knew more than he was saying and he was leaving something unspoken, but she did not know how to pry it from him. She almost had the feeling he was protecting her somehow, or thought he was.

Well, she thought as she pushed away all the questions and thought about the coming night, she would take the hours she had left with him. And she would treasure every last moment.

Chapter Twenty-One

Dougal argued with him, just as he expected, but he gave in and accompanied Rob to his chambers where Lilidh waited. Did she have any idea of the complete catastrophe he'd barely managed to avoid in the hall? Now, his friend trudged up the stairs and along the corridor with him, silent except for an occasional curse aimed at him.

Daft, imbecile, stupid and *bedamned* seemed to be among the ones he favoured for now. It would have been funny, except for the gravity of the whole situation.

Once more Symon had stepped in and caused trouble. This time, keeping Lady MacLerie from leaving nearly resulted in several deaths. Symon's own was only prevented by his unconscious condition—and the chains that bound him in a small room near the kitchens. Rob could take no more chances by leaving him free. Now Lilidh's mother resided with her maid, under guard, until Rob could speak to Duncan in the morning and clear this up. Hopefully, he would find a way to solve the matter of Lilidh MacLerie.

Now he stood before his bedchamber door, not knowing what to expect inside. Had she seen the dagger in her mother's side? Did she hear Symon's threats? Or had Ranald already removed her from it? Dougal whispered something about changing his mind, so Rob lifted the latch and entered alone.

She stood by the window, barely visible in the shadows, staring out into the forest. He walked to her side and watched the flickering lights of the campfires glowing in the night's darkness. He reached up and put his hands on her shoulders, pulling her against him and inhaling the scent of her...while he could.

'What happened, Rob?' she asked. He felt her inhale and hold a breath while waiting for him to answer. He let out the one he'd been holding.

'Symon took your mother prisoner at knife-point.' There really was no way of saying it gently. 'She is well and I've sent word that she will be returned to your cousins on the morrow,' he added.

'May I see her?' she asked.

'Not now. Things have only just settled down. Fear not, she is comfortable and has not been hurt.'

She turned to him and searched his face. 'But you have been hurt.' Lilidh reached up and touched the edge of his jaw where Symon had managed to get a punch in before being subdued.

'I need to speak to you about something important, Lilidh,' he began. 'This becomes more dangerous with each day and…I worry about what will happen to you if this ends badly for me.'

'Rob, you will get us through this, you promised,' she said, stroking his arm now. He smiled at her determination and her faith, especially when his was failing him.

'Dougal is waiting outside. He will be our witness.'

The frown lay across her brow and forehead at his words. He was mucking this up. 'We have had relations. There might be a consequence.'

She shook her head at his words. Then she

realised of what he spoke. 'Why do we need a witness?'

'I would handfast with you in the old ways so that you have the protection of my name if anything happens to me. Dougal has sworn to keep this a secret between us, unless you need to use it.'

'You think you are going to die.'

There were many possibilities, but with the way that he was being undermined, opposed and ignored, most of them were not good outcomes. If she was with child, handfasting would give her some legal protections. If not, they could simply choose to ignore it. He would not hold her to the 'year and a day' tenet and keep her from moving on with her life.

'Things have escalated. If whoever is trying to kill me within the clan does not succeed, there is every possibility that your father will once he hears about our violation in the truce and hospitality we offered.' Rob could still not believe Symon's actions. Once again, his cousin's actions were indefensible.

'But you did not—' she began. He touched his finger to her lips.

'It matters not, Lilidh. I am laird. I am responsible.'

The sound of shuffling feet and a man not trying to be discreet interrupted them. Dougal would
leave soon if he did not open the door.

'Will you, Lilidh? Will you accept the protection I offer and handfast with me?'

He wanted nothing more than to tell her of the
love in his heart for her, but that would make this
something more serious, more permanent, and
he could not offer her that.

Tears filled her beautiful green eyes then
and they trickled down her cheeks when she
nodded. He pulled a length of plaid from the bed
and wrapped it around her shoulders and then
opened the door to let Dougal in.

'My lady,' Dougal said, bowing to her. 'A
strange business in the middle of the night.'

Rob put his arm around Lilidh's shoulders and
took her left hand in his. Clearing his throat, he
tried to say the right words so that they were
bound but not so tightly that she could not escape this as soon as she was safe.

'Lilidh MacLerie, I take you as my wife, before
this witness, and pledge that you have the pro-

tection of my name and this vow for a year and a day,' he said. Dougal handed him a strip of their clan's plaid and he wrapped it around their joined hands. Then he waited for her to say the words.

Her voice came out as a whisper, soft and gentle, as she spoke, her eyes staring into his as she uttered the words of joining.

'Rob Matheson, I take you as my husband, before this witness, and pledge my faithfulness to you and to this vow for a year and a day.' She wrapped the plaid strip once more around their hands and looked up at him. Rob leaned down and kissed her mouth to seal the vows.

'You are both fools and I have witnessed it,' Dougal said, cursing again before he walked away towards the door.

'Thank you, Dougal,' Rob offered, but Dougal left without stopping or looking back.

Rob poured himself some whisky and filled a cup with wine for Lilidh, handing it to her while trying to gauge her reaction to the last few minutes. She walked over and sat on the long bench where she'd sat with her mother earlier.

Dazed and confused. Lovely and exhausted. His wife and the love of his heart.

But that was only temporary and, once any danger was over for her, it would be over, as well.

'What happened at your meeting with Duncan? Did something there cause Symon to act this way?'

'Lilidh, I cannot understand him at all. At times he is reasonable.' At her expression—one of complete disbelief—he laughed and nodded. 'No, truly, sometimes he is quite rational. Then he acts like this, as he did when he kidnapped you, and I am left wondering if he is insane.' He let out a breath. 'And I got the sense that Duncan is delaying. This is not something that should take days of negotiating, but he seems to treat it as such.'

'What good would a delay do, Rob?' she asked, as he sat down next to her and took her hand in his.

He finished his whisky and shook his head. 'It is just a feeling. More than that, I have seen him do this before. He is waiting.' Putting his cup down, he took in the dark circles under her eyes and her pale face and smiled. 'Come. Let us get some rest so that we can face the morrow.'

She allowed him to lead her to the bed. He

tugged the covers loose and held them back for her. His intentions to sleep, just sleep and allow her to, as well, were ruined when she lifted her shift off before climbing in. His body was ready before he reached the other side of the bed.

He tried to take no notice of the call of her passion to his as he placed his weapons on the floor and in the mattress, but by the time he lay at her side, she was impossible to ignore.

She would always be impossible to ignore.

Hell, if he could have, it would have prevented most all of the problems they now faced.

In spite of the willingness of his flesh, he just wanted to hold her this night. To hold her close for this last night.

He fell asleep in minutes, wrapped around her, their bodies entwined. But he woke to find her touching him, skimming her fingers over his skin with her eyes closed as though trying to see him through her touch. Then she opened her eyes and her body and took him inside of her.

This time was unlike any of those before. This joining was slow and easy and left him feeling complete and empty at the same time.

* * *

When the first light of dawn streamed through his window and the sounds of hell arriving at his gate woke them, he knew it was over. The only question was whether or not he would live to see another day.

As he looked out from the battlements at the sea of newly arrived MacLeries and other warriors who were pledged to them, Rob wished someone had summoned the MacKenzies to their side.

They dressed without a word and he took Lilidh down to the chamber where her mother and maid were before gathering with his men and facing the enemy.

Still stunned over the events of the night, Lilidh woke next to Rob with a profound sadness in her heart. Their last time together, something she never thought would ever happen at all, was over and now she would have to face living her life without him. She understood that nothing could or would come of the vows they'd spoken, but that he thought of her safety touched her deeply.

Now, as she walked at his side towards the chamber where her mother was being held, she could not help it if her hand lingered in his grasp, or if she stood too close to him. When the door opened, Rob informed them of his plans.

'Lady MacLerie, if you would follow me now, I'll take you back to your men.'

'I am taking my daughter with me,' she demanded. Standing up to Rob was most likely no problem for the woman who had tamed the *Beast*.

'You will take the maid with you,' he said. Calling out to a few men in the corridor, Rob gave orders that Isla was to be released along with her mother.

A flurry of activity followed as the men carried Isla out of the keep and Rob began to leave, escorting her mother away.

'Remain here until I call for you,' he said, the lover disappearing as the commander and chief were needed.

'Rob,' she said. There were so many things she needed to say to him.

'I will send for you,' he whispered as he pulled the door closed.

And then he was gone.

Chapter Twenty-Two

With his men behind him, Rob led Jocelyn towards the gates.

When Connor arrived this morn, Rob understood why Duncan was delaying—either he knew or suspected that Connor would not stand back and let anyone handle it for him. In a way, though the danger was high, he would finally speak to Connor for the first time in more than four years. If he had doubted it, Connor's voice yelling out his name over his wall confirmed it.

Dougal held the lady in place behind Rob and Rob nodded for one of the wooden-gate doors to be opened. With guards in position to both defend it and ready to close it immediately if the need arose, Rob walked forwards and found Connor standing on the other side of it.

'Laird Matheson,' he said in the booming voice

that spread fear and terror in those who opposed him, 'you have something of mine.'

Rob nodded and Dougal walked Jocelyn forwards. Connor drew his sword, but Rob only placed his hand on his, leaving it in the scabbard for now. Both of them cursed him under their breaths as they passed him. Connor reached out and grabbed Jocelyn, pulling her roughly to him and kissing her before they spoke in whispers. A moment later, Jocelyn sent him a dark glare and walked into the throng of MacLerie warriors.

'And my daughter,' Connor called out once more. When Rob did not react, the Beast of the Highlands continued. 'I will put this keep to the torch and tear it down stone by stone if you do not return my daughter now.' He advanced a few paces until he stood but inches from the entrance—outside the wall but not by much.

Try as he might, when confronted by the man who was more father to him than his own had been and while he looked at the man who had had as much a hand in destroying Lilidh's spirit and life as he himself had, Rob could not stop himself. Although he'd sworn that his clan's needs came first, his need for vengeance or absolution sparked the anger in his blood and he could not simply acquiesce to his mentor now. He stepped closer and spoke in a lower voice so that none would hear it but Connor.

'I think not. For if you harm one Matheson this day, your beloved daughter will discover your part in what played out four years ago.'

A bleak expression entered Connor's eyes and was gone in a second. 'You have not told her?' he asked.

'I will let her think what she might, as long as you pay the gold as demanded and leave.'

'Gold?' Connor laughed. 'So this is more about your greediness and less about your honour, as I suspected.' Rob's hand tightened on the pommel of his sword and he fought not to pull it free and strike.

'And there is one more condition,' Rob added.

'Another?' Connor asked. 'I am not certain you are in a position to make any more demands.'

'I am. I hold your daughter and you want her kept in ignorance of the way you forced me to disavow her. You do not want her to know that you demanded I humiliate her so that there was no hope of a future together. You do not want

Jocelyn to know either. And they will unless you seem to find an *honourable* way to end this now.'

When Connor let out a breath, he looked much older than Rob had ever realised. And more vulnerable. 'You will seek no retribution against my clan for this incident. When you leave, when Lilidh leaves, it is over between us.'

Somehow Rob knew he would accept. Under it all, this beast of a man loved his wife and his daughter and would give anything to protect them. And if it was from the truth of his failings or from the truth of his past actions in this matter, Connor would do it. Rob began to walk away, intending to get Lilidh himself, when Connor delivered a blow as only he could.

'I have a condition as well, Matheson.'

The air thick with foreboding, Rob faced Lilidh's father and waited to hear it.

'You must end it completely with her. As you did before. I will not have her pining away, thinking something will come of this.'

Rob closed his eyes for a moment, trying to ignore the screaming in his heart and soul. If he was going to be laird here, if he was going to be worthy enough to be chief and command the respect and loyalty of his kin, then he must be loyal to them. If he did as Connor demanded, his clan would be left unmolested and able to ally themselves elsewhere. If he did not, Connor would return and destroy them later.

If he was going to be the leader he must be, he had to let her go completely.

Again.

Turning away, he began walking back to the keep. Dougal followed him, whispering furiously, but Rob waved him off. He walked through the silent hall and the kitchens to the chamber where she waited for him. Opening the door, he prepared to do something he'd regret until his last breath to the woman he loved.

'Lilidh, your father waits for you at the gates,' he said. 'Your things are already there.'

She began shaking her head at him. 'Rob, let me speak to him. This can be worked out. You were willing to handfast with me and I am certain he will accept—'

'It is over, Lilidh. Now, come with me.'

He did not wait for her to argue more, he simply took her by the arm and led her out. He kept the pace a quick one so that she would have to concentrate on her path and her leg and not be able to continue to argue with him. A cowardly thing to do, but it was a kindness compared to what he must do next.

They crossed the yard and made their way to the gate where Connor yet stood, unmoved in the time since Rob left him there. Only his eyes betrayed any emotion when he caught sight of Lilidh approaching. Steeling himself for what he must do, he released her arm a few paces from the gate.

'Rob. Father. We should speak in private,' Lilidh began.

'There is no need for that now, Lilidh. Your father will take you home now,' he said.

'But, Rob, we have—' He knew she would reveal the vows, so he interrupted her and began his descent into the hell his life would be.

'We have spent memorable hours together, my sweet. I will miss having you to warm my bed,' he said, adding a coarse laugh to his words. 'I was happy to oblige a widow's need for such things, but nothing else can exist for us. Your father understands I accepted what you offered me, but now I must wed as my clan directs. Tyra has waited long enough.'

She gasped and began to sway. 'Rob, you said—'

'Well, Laird MacLerie,' he called out as he pushed her towards Connor, 'you have your daughter. Where is the gold?'

Lilidh stumbled the few steps until she reached her father. He pulled her close and whispered something to her that Rob could not hear. Then he called to one of his soldiers, who carried a chest forwards. Connor took the chest and tossed it at Rob's feet.

'Your gold, Laird Matheson.'

Rob stood frozen as the sound of Lilidh's soft cries echoed across the yard. Connor led her to the centre of his men and Rob ordered the gates closed. He could not speak to anyone right now or he would begin to beg for her forgiveness and her love, so he climbed the steps to the top of the wall and watched the MacLeries begin to leave.

Three hours later, when the midday sun reached high overhead, they were gone.

At the evening meal that night, one he did not eat, the elders toasted the way he'd handled the

MacLerie laird, they toasted their good will and they toasted him as a worthy son to the late laird.

But Rob had never felt more unworthy than he did now—for he had failed once more to stand up as a man to Connor MacLerie. And he'd hurt Lilidh more deeply than she deserved.

How she got home, she never knew, for one minute she stood in Keppoch Keep thinking of ways to convince her father to accept her vows with Rob and the next she lay in the same chamber where she had slept before her marriage. Lilidh remembered bits and pieces of the journey, but very little after Rob humiliated her again with his easy dismissal of their time together.

Of their love.

Her siblings and cousins visited her to welcome her home throughout the next week. Her father occasionally informed her of letters from the MacGregors, asking after her and about her recovery from the unfortunate incident. Other than that, she could not face him. Twice she'd been a fool to believe Rob's word and twice he'd humiliated her in front of her father.

Even when she found him watching her expectantly, she could not speak to him. Her mother spent time with her and never mentioned Rob or the time that she'd been at Keppoch...

Or the passion they shared.

Or the love that he swore and then disavowed.

Or the way he'd made her feel whole once and again.

Shaking off her despondency was difficult because he returned to her in her dreams and she woke sobbing in despair or shuddering in pleasure as her body and soul remembered every moment of it. Lilidh became a master of deception in those next weeks—deceiving herself and others that it had mattered not to her.

She spent her days reading or sewing and ignoring the devastation in her heart. She spent her nights dreaming of being back in his arms.

To get away from some of the pitying glances, she began spending time in the village with her cousin Ciara, who was awaiting the birth of her second child. Since she could no longer travel with her father on the laird's business, Ciara did any work in her home, one built by Ciara's husband, Tavis.

Ciara was intelligent and had a similar sense

of humour as Lilidh had, so it was a wonderful diversion to spend days with her. And it was a chance comment by Ciara, about two weeks after Lilidh's return to Lairig Dubh, that made her realise her courses had not come.

And that she was carrying Rob's bairn.

Chapter Twenty-Three

Rob had spent the weeks after Lilidh's departure picking up the pieces of his life and moving on. His respite from the reality he must face was over, as was any hope of ever correcting his past errors in judgement or behaviour.

Now that the elders supported him, Rob had had Symon released, but still watched. Without a conflict or danger expected from the MacLeries, Rob had begun to discuss a formal treaty with the MacKenzies. The large, powerful clan had much to offer their smaller one, he had told himself for the thousandth time. It did not lessen the disloyalty he felt as he discussed the matter and planned to move forwards on it.

Because so much of his life had been tied to the MacLeries, he still had to struggle to let go of the desire to be part of them. Not that he could.

Not with what he had done to Lilidh again. So he lived this farce until one night when he finally came to his senses, but nearly lost his head.

Rob heard his name being whispered and roused from his sleep to it. Tyra knelt next to him in his bed with a long, dangerous blade at his throat.

'I am tired of dealing with fools, Rob,' she said. The dagger shook in her hand as she leaned in towards him. 'You have interfered for the last time.' He tried to sit up, but she pushed the lethal tip into the skin of his neck.

Looking at her now, he realised he was looking into the face of madness.

'How have I interfered, Tyra? Tell me so we can come to some accommodation.' That seemed to calm her agitation somewhat, so he continued. 'What do you want me to do?' He held up his hands and began to edge away from her.

'You were supposed to die. You were supposed to die,' she repeated, almost in a chant. 'Why did you have to return at all? Why did you not die?' Many things fell into place in that moment, including his failure to realise that Tyra was behind Symon's strange actions.

'Tyra,' he said softly, glancing towards the door and hoping someone had seen her coming here. 'Let me get dressed and we can figure this all out.' Once he was out of the bed, he could take the dagger, but not now in this position. All it would take would be a slight press and he'd bleed to death.

'Symon should be laird. I can control him,' she said, nodding her head. 'I did control him until you interfered.'

'Why not call Symon and we can all speak about this matter?' he offered. With her leaning over as she was, any sudden move on his part would send her in a downward motion—blade first.

'I already summoned him. You will be dead when he gets here, but I'll make certain he is blamed for it. Then both of you are out of my way.'

Holy Christ! Symon must have outlived his usefulness to her, too. He had to keep her talking until he could make a move.

'What will you do then, Tyra? Surely you must have a plan?' He tried to let his body relax next to her, hoping she would lean back away a bit.

'With the new treaty signed and our alliance with the MacKenzies in place, I will marry Gavin as we have always planned.'

'Marry Gavin?' he asked. He knew Gavin and he knew that Gavin was betrothed to an heiress from Sutherland. They might already be married.

'We have planned it for years. My father began talks with his father long ago. With your death, the betrothal you tried to arrange for us is gone and I am free to marry him.'

Rob saw a flicker of movement behind her and realised someone else was in the bedchamber with them. Deciding it was time, he glanced directly over her shoulder.

'Symon,' he said, without knowing who it was there. As he'd hoped, it distracted her enough that he could push and the person behind her could pull her before she could cut his throat.

It was Symon indeed and he pushed his sister to the floor and grabbed the dagger from her hands as she screamed. Then he turned the blade in his palm and aimed it once more at Rob.

Out of the girdle pan and into the flames below? he wondered.

Then Symon flipped the dagger and held it out

to him, grip first. Rob got out of the bed and called for guards. When he got back, Symon had pulled Tyra to her feet. She'd quieted somewhat, but her whispered murmurings disturbed him. Seeing Symon through new eyes, Rob realised he'd been misdirected to suspect him by his mad sister and her irrational plans.

'Take her down to the storage room and keep her there until we figure this out,' he said. 'I will get one of the women to stay with her this night.'

'I will stay with her, Rob,' Symon said.

'I think we need to talk, Symon.' The guards arrived and escorted them both away.

With the crisis averted and the real villain exposed, it still took days and weeks to sort things out. Only a thorough search of Tyra's belongings, both those in plain sight and those they were able to find hidden away, revealed the extent of her dangerous delusions. Rob was lucky that he and Lilidh had not been killed as she'd planned. Listening to her nearly incoherent ramblings and rantings made it clear that his father and Aileen had been victims of her deranged violence. Her father might have been, as well.

Symon and he came to terms. Though a hot-headed pain in the arse, Rob was glad he had not been involved in Tyra's plans after all. The elders seemed pleased with that, as well, and he was welcomed to the council when he returned from taking Tyra to a cousin who was the abbess at a convent. She would be confined there and not able to hurt anyone else.

And, after he exchanged some messages with Gavin MacKenzie, Rob felt certain that the man had played no part in this other than to have treated a young woman kindly. Tyra's twisted mind had ascribed all kinds of things to that kindness, even forging letters that turned Gavin into her co-conspirator, in her mind.

Two months after Lilidh left him, his life was back to what it had been before Symon brought her here and the clan was safe. Things had never looked more promising for the Clan Matheson. Or so empty for its laird.

Rob was standing on the battlements in front of the ruined tower when Dougal brought him the letter.

Jocelyn MacLerie had written him once more.

* * *

'I am just tired, Mother,' Lilidh explained. 'I'm afraid I walked too much yesterday and my leg is suffering for it.'

Her mother grew suspicious, she knew, but Lilidh just could not speak to her about her condition yet. After she missed her courses once, she waited for their return. Now, she'd missed twice and, along with other signs and symptoms, she knew there was no mistake—she was pregnant.

And though she'd not confided in Ciara, she knew her cousin had guessed the truth, as well.

'We will have visitors coming in a few days, Lilidh,' her mother said. 'The Murrays from Perth,' she explained. James Murray's wife, Elizabeth, was a MacLerie and had grown up as friends with Ciara and Lilidh. After their shocking elopement at the time of Ciara and Tavis's marriage, Elizabeth and James visited several times a year.

'It will be good to see Elizabeth,' Lilidh admitted. 'I was not here for her last visit.'

Her marriage to Iain had just taken place and she'd left for his lands before the Murrays arrived. Elizabeth could not travel sooner and missed her wedding because of the impending birth of their first child.

Jocelyn emptied the solar with a simple nod of her head and Lilidh found herself dreading the coming minutes. There was no way to avoid it, and, if she was being honest with herself, Lilidh would have admitted she needed her mother's counsel.

'So, do you plan to tell Rob you carry his child or not?' her mother asked.

'Do I?'

'Well, the lovely green shade of your skin in the morning nearly matches your eyes and you have been seeking your rest every day after the noon meal.' Her mother's eyes narrowed then and Lilidh prepared for the worst. 'And your monthly courses have gone missing since your return here. Since you mentioned in your letter that you carried no heir for Iain, that means...' Her mother didn't finish the rest—there was no need.

'No, I do not,' she finally said in reply to the first question.

'It is his child, Lilidh. He should know.' Her mother came over to her and knelt down before her. 'What will you do?'

'I do not know,' she whispered. 'Father will be furious.' Her biggest fear.

'You could go to stay with Elizabeth until the bairn is born.' Lilidh met her mother's eyes. *And return after the birth...alone* was the unspoken part.

'One choice, yes,' she said.

'We could arrange a marriage,' her mother offered another. 'Many families clamour to align themselves with the MacLeries.'

And would not look too closely at her condition coming to the marriage, also unspoken.

'Another choice.'

'If you are certain there is nothing between you and Rob?' Her mother was relentless when she wanted to know something.

Lilidh pushed out of her chair and walked to the window that overlooked the yard. Watching those who lived in Lairig Dubh go about their day, she shrugged, finally letting the anger she'd felt escape.

'Why would I want him, Mother?' She clenched her hands into fists as it spilled out. 'He humiliated me, not once, but twice, before my family and his. I know he did not plan my kidnapping and he made no promises about a life together, but he did not hesitate to accept my—'

'Love?' her mother offered.

'Favours. Advice. Help,' she finished instead. 'He swore that he'd been young and stupid the first time. He said it was not about my...scars. And then he did it again.' The tears overflowed her eyes and trickled down her face. She brushed them away before looking at her mother. 'He did it again.'

'That is more than you've said about him since you returned with us.'

'It hurts, Mother. It hurts.' Her mother opened her arms and wrapped Lilidh in a hug.

'Of course it does. Loving someone is not easy.'

She would have argued, but why? She could not deny she loved him—loved him in spite of everything—but that did not mean she would act the fool in this and beg him. Handfasting aside, he did not deserve to know about this bairn. Her hand moved across her still-flat belly.

'I think you should speak to your father soon about this, Lilidh. He should learn of it from you and not through rumours, as he will if you delay.'

'I know,' she said, nodding. 'I have other questions to ask him, about something Rob said, but I just cannot bring myself to do it.'

'What about Rob?' her mother asked. 'Mayhap I can help you? He was my foster son, too.'

'Ah, yes,' she said, laughing softly then. 'You were in charge of teaching him correct manners.' She knew her mother remembered her encounter and comment to Rob about remembering his manners and losing his wits. 'There is something that happened, between him and Father, that he would not speak of. I suspect Father will not, either.'

'Why not ask him?' her father said from behind them. How could so large a man be so quiet when he wanted to sneak up on someone? He kissed her on the forehead and rubbed her back. 'What is it you wish to know?'

Did she dare? Did she want to know the truth, no matter what? Yes, she did.

'What happened when Rob came to you for permission to marry me?' she asked.

Her mother gasped and turned to her father. 'Connor? Pray tell me he did not!' Her tall, dangerous father wore a sheepish expression now and

Lilidh knew she would find out the truth. 'Rob asked for her hand?'

'Aye, he did.' Her father looked from her to her mother and back again. 'I said no.'

'When? You never told me he had,' her mother asked now. When her father hesitated, her mother grabbed his arm and tugged on it. Deciding that her mother could wring more truth from him than she could, Lilidh waited silently for it to be revealed.

'He came to me after I'd heard talk of what you two were doing together. Running wild, being seen together too much, then he was overheard boasting about...' He paused and met her gaze then. 'Enjoying your favours, Lilidh. He boasted of what the two of you did together.'

'We were pledged!' she cried out.

'Pledged? I gave permission for no such thing. He overstepped the boundaries I set for him.' He crossed his arms across his massive chest and glared at her. 'He was too low for you to consider as a match.'

'Because he is a bastard?' she challenged.

'Because he is unworthy of you!' he yelled back. His words surprised her, partly because of the word but more so because of the vehemence.

'Unworthy? He came to you as a foster son and you accepted him. You trained him as a warrior and as a man. He would not take my honour, Father, before our marriage. I offered, he refused! Then he came to you, seeking the honourable way.'

'And when I refused it, he left.'

'He did not simply leave, Connor,' her mother said softly. 'Please tell me you had nothing to do with the manner in which he...broke from Lilidh.'

No words were needed, for the guilt was written boldly across his face. Lilidh gasped, feeling sick and faint. 'You made him do that? How? Why?'

'I challenged him. I told him he had disobeyed me and my orders. I'd told him you were no bitch for him to sniff after. But he disobeyed me and broke our bond.' His voice quieted then for the rest of it. 'I told him it would be war if he did not break things cleanly and completely with you. In a way that would guarantee you would not want anything to do with him again.'

'Oh, dear God in Heaven!' her mother cried.

'And he did it, did he not? If he had been worthy of you, he would have told me to go to hell and claimed you. But he didn't.'

'Connor, he was just a boy.'

'Old enough to be involved with my daughter,' he said.

'He would never have stood up to you. Your men fear you. He was too young.' Even she could hear the sadness in her mother's voice. Sadness and disappointment, not in Rob, but in her father. Lilidh understood she was witnessing something between them she'd never seen before.

'He had another chance and, once more, he did not choose you, Lilidh. He chose his clan and my gold instead of you,' he explained. 'He is still not worthy of you.'

Her stomach rolled then and she knew she was going to be sick. Whether the bairn or the facts she'd just learned, it mattered not the cause. Without a word, she raced from the solar and sought her chambers.

Lilidh discovered that her chambers were the worst place for her to seek relief from the pounding in her head or the piercing pain of her breaking heart. Something she'd not thought possible since that terrible day long ago—carrying Rob's child—was now a reality and was now her responsibility to handle. To her shame, part of her would have taken Rob back this moment if he returned to her and asked. Another warring part made her spine stiffen and her chin tilt up and want to refuse him no matter her condition. But now, now there was a bairn to consider, another life—her child's—to care for and that put this in a different light for her.

Walking to the battlements above her chambers, she stood, eyes closed, allowing the winds to buffet her along until she reached the corner. The fact that it was her parents' favourite place to stand and watch the yard below was not missed by her and she waited for some idea, some plan, to strike her.

Hours later, her head was clear but her heart was no less heavy than before. But since Rob had had two months to come back to her, if he was going to do it, she had little choice but to look elsewhere for solutions to her dilemma.

And once more, her heart would bear the cost of giving her love to a man who wished it not.

Chapter Twenty-Four

Silence surrounded them for several minutes. Connor went and poured himself a large cup of whisky and, after offering it to her first, drank it down. He sat down on one of the benches there. She was so angry at him that she could not even look at him.

He'd always been overbearing and controlling and a hard man, a beast, but this was worse. This was…hateful. And Jocelyn just could not understand why. If he objected to Rob because he was baseborn, so be it. But he'd accepted Rob and brought him up as part of their household and never treated him as such. At this moment, though, she cared not. She was so angry that she wanted to…

'Do you think she'll ever tell me about the bairn?' he asked in a low voice.

Somehow he knew. It should not surprise her, but it did. Was that what had brought him to the solar in the middle of the day?

'I doubt it,' she said, still not meeting his gaze.

'Did you speak about what she can do about this?' She heard something creeping into his voice then—pain? Doubt?

'Yes. I gave her several things to think about. The Murrays' visit might be fortuitous for her.'

'Jocelyn,' he began in that tone that would tear out her heart. She shook her head and walked to the door.

'I am so angry with you that I cannot speak about it now. I will see you at dinner.'

Jocelyn left him in the solar and went to find Lilidh.

The only thing that lightened her mood was knowing that she'd already sent her note on its way. If she was not as furious, she might have explained her reasons to her husband. But not now—she was *that* angry that she decided she would not tell him at all.

Connor sat back and watched Jocelyn leave. She was right—damn her!—too much of the time and this was another of those times. He'd thought about his actions those four years ago and realised he was wrong.

When the first rumours were reported to him, he'd had a long talk with Rob about Lilidh's future and his own and how they would go along different paths. Mostly because her marriage would be used to make or strengthen political alliances and he would not rise to that level as the illegitimate son of the Matheson with others ahead of him to inherit and lead. But Connor understood the passions of youth and had hoped he impressed on Rob the boundaries of his behaviour.

Then more specific things were reported back to him—Rob's lewd boasts to his friends about the way it was between him and Lilidh. The boundaries were being pushed and so Connor spoke to him again, talking about honour and loyalty and obedience. He'd even spoken to Lilidh about the same matters, but he knew she was attracted to the young handsome boy in their midst. Connor had recognised, as a father and a man, the glimmer of first love in her gaze and it had scared him.

So, when Rob came to him to ask his permission to speak to his father about a betrothal, Connor exploded with an insulting challenge to see if he would rise above himself and stand up for what he wanted, for who he wanted.

Instead, Rob did every outrageous thing he demanded in trying to pacify him into not starting war with his clan and to save himself from the humiliation of being disgraced as the cause of it. When Connor told him to make it look as though he was rejecting Lilidh, the boy did it.

Worse, the terrible mistake escalated and there was no way back from it. It caused a break in the long friendship Connor had had with Angus and left them both bitter and angry over it.

Now, four years later, there were even more repercussions from his stupid decision and actions.

Now, Rob still believed himself unworthy because of his actions. Connor just prayed the boy would see the truth before it was too late.

'And what exactly do you think is going to happen?' Dougal asked him as they walked up the steps to Rob's chambers.

'I will not repeat the past, Dougal. I have lived

as though Connor's words to me were true. I will not do it any longer.'

'So,' he asked as they entered the bedchambers filled with thousands of memories now for Rob, 'you think the MacLeries will just let you ride off with Lilidh? Do you think she will even speak to her after what you said? What you did?'

Miserable after two months without her, Rob knew he had been a fool. And he had been as unworthy of Lilidh as her father had accused. He'd let Connor scare him off four years ago, doing the laird's dirty work for him on the way out, but no more.

These last two months had been hell.

So many times he returned here to share something with her or to get her opinion or to discuss a plan, only to realise she was gone. He'd chased her away in spite of the love she had given to him.

Because of his fears.

What the hell kind of laird could he be if he was ruled by fear?

'Rob,' Dougal said, grabbing his arm to make him stop packing, 'the elders are not in favour of this either.'

'I do not give a damn whether they like it or

not. If I am laird, I will decide. If they do not want me as laird, there is always Symon.' He stopped a moment or two later when he noticed the horrified expression on his friend's face. 'I ask you again—will you come with me?'

'And do what?' Dougal crossed his arms and glared at him.

'Pick up the pieces of my body and bring them back for burial?' he asked. Though he said it in jest, it was one possibility of what could happen to him at the hands of the MacLeries. 'Guard my back.'

'If I was guarding your back, I would convince you of the folly of such an action. Let some time pass before approaching them. Send a message or two to gauge their willingness to talk. Use an intermediary to establish talks.'

Rob held out the parchment then, letting his friend read it. It was similar wording to the one from a year ago, but this time he had received it.

My husband is seeking an appropriate match for Lilidh's hand in marriage.

'There is no time,' Rob said. 'I leave at first light.'

Dougal looked from the message to Rob and

back again before letting out a loud sigh. 'You know he'll send Rurik up against you first. Can you defeat him in battle?'

Could he defeat the MacLerie's champion? The largest and strongest man he had ever met? Could he?

The answer, as he discovered just a week later, was no.

Rurik was as unbeatable now as he'd always been. As Rob forced himself up from the ground for the fourth time, he reminded himself of why he was doing this.

For her. For Lilidh.

Yet, he had not seen or heard her. Barely through the gates of Lairig Dubh, Rurik had charged him. Dougal had been dragged aside and now the battle went on through the yard. It was hard to see who observed them since one eye was swollen closed. It was hard to breathe with the broken ribs Rurik had caused with the first punch delivered. The blood streaming down his leg from the gash there made the ground underneath it slippery.

He'd begun fully armed with his sword, targe

and dagger. As Rurik circled him now, only the sword was left. When those in the yard stopped cheering for Rurik and taunting him, Rob knew that Connor had arrived.

'What are you doing here, Matheson?' Connor called out. Rob turned in the direction of the call, hoping he faced Connor, but not certain because he could not see well.

'I am here for Lilidh,' he answered back, wondering if she was watching this and cheering for Rurik.

'You are not worthy of her. Go home and do not return here.'

'I think I am, MacLerie. I will not leave without her.'

The quiet at his approach now gave way to complete and utter silence, only the sounds of his hard breathing breaking into it. He'd challenged their laird—something few men had done and lived to tell of it. Thinking about it, the only man he knew who had was the one who had greeted him—Rurik.

'Then show me how worthy you are, Matheson.'

The gauntlet had been thrown now. Rob would

have to take her father down to prove himself to all the MacLeries. But even that did not guarantee Lilidh would accept him. This was just the next step in what would undoubtedly be the most painful experience of his life. Well, he thought as he took in as deep a breath as his chest would allow, she was worth it.

That was the last coherent thought for some time as he charged across in Connor's direction and attacked. He gave it his all—never giving ground, never slowing, always moving forwards. He swung that sword until his arms screamed and until he could barely draw a breath. The noise overwhelmed him—so loud that it sounded like an army in a pitched battle around him. Or that might be because Connor had struck his head with the hilt of his sword and his ears were ringing.

He knew from the grunts that he had hit Connor several times, though the man never slowed down or tried to evade him. He only thought about Lilidh as he struggled to keep up.

Then, somehow, he managed to catch hold of Connor's sword and fling it away with his. The crowd roared again, but he did not waste time listening. He chased Connor down and ploughed into him, knocking him to the ground as he tried to grab for the sword. Though he was certain his shoulder came out of its socket from the force with which he landed on Connor, he swung around and pinned Connor on the ground. Then, with his sword at Connor's neck, he demanded his surrender.

Instead of hearing the words, he heard swords being drawn around him. MacLerie warriors surrounded him and pointed their swords at him now—killing their laird simply would not be allowed, whether he'd won or not. He put his hand up then and dropped his sword. Connor climbed to his feet and strode up to him, to deliver the death blow, no doubt.

'Tell her I tried,' Rob said quietly to Connor.

'Tell her yourself,' Connor growled back, looking over Rob's shoulder towards the keep. Rob forced his battered and bleeding body to turn.

She looked like an angel, her hair streaming out behind her as she moved towards him. Her mouth opened and suddenly he realised it was not an angel—she was the legendary *bean-shithe*, the fairy woman whose scream foretold one's death. Men moved out of her path in fear that she shrieked for them.

By the time the creature reached him, he thought it was Lilidh, but his open eye blurred from the blood dripping into it from a cut somewhere above it. He tried to reach out for her, but his arm would not obey. She stood before him now and he was grateful that the last thing he saw in this life would be her face.

Then the ground reached up and pulled him down to meet it.

Chapter Twenty-Five

The sting of frigid water woke him and he coughed and choked on it, sending slashes of pain throughout his beaten body. But the pain told him he yet lived.

Forcing his one eye open, he saw Connor and Jocelyn standing above him. The lady was whispering furiously at her husband, who did not seem to be listening at all. Tilting his head back, he recognised the curtain of black silk that cascaded around him—Lilidh's hair. He wanted to tangle his fingers in it, but one hand would still not obey him and the other was holding hers.

'Give me your hand, boy,' Rurik said, reaching down for him. Though Lilidh began to argue and Jocelyn, he noticed, turned away, there was no way to avoid the warrior who grabbed his useless hand and pulled it. The sky above him flashed white and the very fires of hell coursed through his body as Rurik put his shoulder back in place.

'Good fight, boy,' Rurik said with a nod in his direction. 'I would not have thought it in you,' he added as he walked past.

When Rob could sit up, he noticed that Connor did not look unscathed and he felt some satisfaction in that. He might not have won, but he had given as good as he got. Connor nodded his head at Rob and he found himself hauled to his feet by two guards.

'Go away,' Connor ordered loudly.

The yard, now that he could see it, cleared at the laird's orders, leaving only the four of them.

'You are not the boy you were then, Rob,' Connor said, gruffly.

Jocelyn whispered something to him and pushed against his arm. Connor held out his hand to Rob. Rob took it, wincing at the power in the older man's grip.

'I want your blessing, Connor. I would have Lilidh to wife if she will have me,' he insisted, not looking at Lilidh for fear he would lose his nerve then.

'If she will have you,' Connor said, releasing

his hand and putting his arm around his wife. 'I was wrong about you, Rob. I was wrong.'

That was as close to an apology as Rob was going to get, but he did not care right now. Lilidh yet held on to his other hand and had not moved from his side. Connor grabbed his wife's hand and tugged her in the direction of the keep. 'Come into the hall and tell us if we have a wedding to prepare or not,' Lilidh's father called back to them.

Rob lifted their clasped hands up and kissed hers. The bloody mark he left from his split lip was not the most romantic thing he could have done, but she seemed not to notice it. Though he dripped water on her, she leaned against him.

'I am sorry it took so long to understand your advice, Lilidh.'

'My advice?' she asked. Then a smile lit her face and he knew she was going to laugh. 'You listened to my advice?'

'These last months I could hear your words in my head. But I want to hear them from you. I want you to help me be the laird and chief I can be—not the one my father was or your father is.' He kissed her gently and then added something

that he had never said aloud to her. 'I am so sorry
for what I did to you, what I said. I understand if
you hate me for the cruel words, but I hope you
will forgive me and give me another chance. I
love you, Lilidh, and I want you for ever, not just
a year and a day.'

She kissed his face then, feathering light, gentle
kisses across all the cuts and bruises he now wore
and he lost himself in the love she showed him.

'I forgive you, Rob,' she whispered to him, easing the tightness in his chest that had nothing to
do with the fight he'd just survived.

'And you will have me? For ever?' he asked,
hoping that her answer was the one he hoped it
would be.

'Yes, my love. For ever.'

He would have to wait to show her how happy it
made him, for the air around him began to shim-
mer and sparkle and the ground began to move
back up at him. The good thing was that having
her at his side slowed his descent and he landed
with less of a thud than the first time.

'Rob!' she cried out, waking him from his stupor.

'I am well,' he answered though his body rebelled at the lie. He did not want to think of the number of broken bones or bruises or cuts on him. He just wanted to think about her.

'Is this a good time to tell you something else?' she said, as she brushed the hair back out of his eyes and caressed his cheek.

'What is it?'

'I think my parents will want a wedding quickly, Rob.'

'Do you not want to wait and have one they have time to prepare for? Is that not what every woman wants?' he asked, feeling the blood whooshing around inside his ears.

'If we do not marry soon, people will be counting back and calling our bairn a seven-month babe.'

It took a few moments for the news to rattle through his brain and make sense, but when it did, he pulled her close and kissed her breathless.

Well, he tried, but then he began coughing and groaning from the pain. 'You carry my child now?' he asked.

She smiled and nodded. 'Are you pleased?'

For a moment, a vision of her blossoming under his watch, filled with his child, was all he could see.

'I am very pleased, Lilidh.'

That was the last thing he remembered until he woke in her bed in the keep two days later.

Chapter Twenty-Six

The bride was radiant, or tried to be, everyone agreed, even though her face was a ghastly shade of green as she walked up to meet her husband. The ceremony had already been delayed by her sudden bouts of illness. Though most of the men thought it must be her nerves, all the women recognised it for what it was.

The groom looked worse for the wear, but so did the bride's father who escorted her forwards and presented her before the priest. The Matheson laird limped and held his chest during some of the ceremony and he had difficulty leaning over to sign the contracts when they were presented to him.

None of his family was present, save one cousin who stood as his witness. That one seemed to be the only one enjoying himself, for he frequently laughed aloud at the groom's moans and groans.

The vows were spoken, rings and kisses exchanged and the priest declared them married and husband and wife. Before clapping or cheering could begin, the bride bolted for a bucket and several people found it difficult to keep their own food down at the sound of her retching.

'Bad food, do you think?' Duncan, the MacLerie negotiator, asked his wife in a joking tone from where they stood in the back of the church.

Marian slapped him and laughed. 'I think not,' she answered, as they all remembered her condition on their wedding day.

'I did not think he would come for her,' Rurik said.

'Did you have to be so harsh to him?' his wife Margriet asked. 'And then he faced Connor as well? No wonder he is still limping.'

'I did not damage any of his important bits,' Rurik said.

'Rurik, not here,' his wife chided.

The group followed the procession back over to the keep where a feast had been prepared. If this wedding was last minute or rushed, no one complained. Duncan had little trouble drawing up the marriage contracts and getting both lairds to accept them. Lilidh brought a handsome dowry to her new husband, along with a renewed bond between their families. Too late to mend the rift between Connor and his old friend Angus, but soon enough to allow Lilidh and Rob their happiness.

Some time later, fulfilling their tradition of being last in their hall, Connor and Jocelyn joined them at table where they raised a cup and sent up a cheer for the newly married couple. After a few cups were shared and the hall grew quiet, Connor finally spoke about the past.

'I was wrong all those years ago,' he said.

'Something you do not usually admit,' Jocelyn said.

'Something he never admits,' Duncan added, holding up his cup in a mock salute.

'The night is late and we should seek our beds,' Rurik said, beginning to rise from his seat.

'Not so quickly, Rurik,' Margriet said. 'We need to discuss the wager.'

Connor was suspiciously silent, as was Jocelyn.

'I understand why Connor is not boasting of our victory in this match, the women always thought they would make a good match,' Duncan explained.

'Her marriage to Iain was a good one. They seemed happy,' Connor added, trying not to lose completely.

'Jocelyn,' Rurik said, 'you are strangely quiet about this.'

Duncan watched as the woman he'd brought for his laird long ago blushed. 'What have you done?'

'I...cheated!' she said with a laugh and a guilty glance thrown in her husband's direction.

The mother of the bride was not supposed to interfere, but apparently Jocelyn had broken that rule and was unrepentant about her violation.

'What did you do?' Marian asked. His wife had tried to influence their daughter's marriage choice, as well. Women, Duncan had discovered long ago, meddled where they were wont to.

'I sent Rob a note about Connor's plans,' she said, looking around the table at them. 'The boy needed a push.'

'Tell them,' Connor growled at her.

'Twice. I sent two notes. Once before the match

with Iain and another when I discovered that Lilidh was…' She stopped before announcing it officially.

'Just so,' Duncan said.

Margriet met their eyes and smiled. 'So this
would appear to be a draw, then—her first marriage was the men's choice, this second one ours.'

'I wonder who will be next?' Connor asked as
he rose and took Jocelyn by the hand. Duncan
could see that the strain between his laird and his
wife seemed to be easing. A good thing, for the
bond between them affected everyone and everything in Lairig Dubh and the strife between
them was too obvious to ignore these last weeks.

'Well, since my daughter and yours are married
now, it would seem only fair if Rurik and Margriet's was next,' Duncan said, taking his own
wife's hand and kissing it. Standing, they looked
down on Rurik and Margriet, who now looked as
though they had both eaten something spoiled.

'I can only pray not,' Margriet, the woman
raised in a convent, said with panic in her eyes.

'Isobel is too young yet to be thinking of this,'
Rurik declared as he crossed his arms over his

chest in a gesture that warned them not to contradict him. None dared argue with him.

But they all knew she was not. And some of them knew that a certain man was already showing an interest in the lovely Isobel Ruriksdotter, though none was brave enough to say so to Rurik's face.

'Be well, friends,' Duncan called out as he and Marian walked hand in hand to their bedchamber. 'The morning will come far too soon.'

And that night, like so many nights, happiness filled the halls of Lairig Dubh.

Epilogue

Keppoch Keep
Three Years Later

'My father does not look happy,' Lilidh whispered to him as they watched the Earl of Douran enter their gates.

Rob turned to glance at Gavin MacKenzie and noticed the same expression on his face. 'Neither is Gavin,' Rob pointed out to his wife.

But there was so much depending on this meeting of two of the wealthiest and most powerful chieftains in the west of Scotland that the lack of mirth did not surprise him. It had taken him more than a year to work out the details and arrangements for this parlay and Rob worried over its success. Lilidh squeezed his hand.

'It will all work out fine, Rob,' she whispered

before letting his hand drop and taking a step back and away from him.

He would allow no such obeisance from her now since any success was in large part due to her efforts as well. No one could force the Beast of the Highlands to do something he was loath to do except for the wife and daughter he loved so much. When Lilidh enlisted her mother's support, Connor had had no choice but to agree.

But his face showed just how much he did not wish to be here.

'Connor, welcome to Keppoch Keep,' he said aloud as he waited for his father-by-marriage to dismount and approach.

Since he was an earl, Rob bowed respectfully as Lilidh curtsied and they waited for Connor's signal to rise. Considering that Gavin MacKenzie was of lower rank and bowing as well, Rob almost laughed as Connor dragged out the moment much longer than was customary. Then he watched as Connor gained power over his adversary, as he'd done many, many times before.

'Connor, may I introduce you to the MacKenzie? Gavin...' Rob said, turning to the younger chieftain. 'May I make you known to the Earl of Douran, the MacLerie?'

As expected, Gavin bowed again. 'My Lord Douran.'

A smile played on Lilidh's face now and a matching one tugged the corners of the irascible Connor MacLerie as he let the man remain bowing before him. Then Connor reached out and offered his hand to Gavin and he rose and shook it.

'Come now, Gavin. We are linked by marriage already and hopefully more soon, so please call me Connor. This is my wife, Jocelyn MacCallum, Lady MacLerie.'

He was so predictable in this that Rob found it difficult not to laugh. As the two men introduced their wives and close kin, Rob and Lilidh watched as the first step to the negotiations went smoothly. Then Lilidh invited them all within for the prepared meal and, as the group moved into the keep, Rob tugged Lilidh's hand to keep her at his side.

'Does he never use a different greeting?' he asked her in a low tone so none would hear.

'Only for someone higher in noble or royal status than he,' she whispered back. 'It is successful in reminding others of their lower status, so he continues.'

They reached the dais and he watched as his steward guided everyone to the appropriate seats, which only long discussions and strategic planning could devise so that none were insulted. Once everyone was seated, both at the high table and those below, Rob took his cup and rose to make his official greeting to all those visiting Keppoch Keep.

But as he held his cup aloft, everything around him seemed to cease. Time itself seemed to pause as he beheld all that he had achieved in his life.

Lilidh's smile, one that held promise and love and passion, reminded him of her support and love since they finally chose each other over everyone else. Now, she carried their second child—a secret she would reveal to her parents during their visit here.

Connor and Jocelyn—his parents for many years—now sat as friends and allies at his table.

His cousin Symon—once his adversary and now the commander of all Matheson warriors— sat next to his wife of a year. Marriage to Mairi MacKenzie had forged a strong bond between their clans, but more importantly, had given Symon the happiness that had been missing from his life for so long.

Gavin MacKenzie and his wife, Edana, were new allies and, with Lilidh's and Rob's efforts to re-establish relations between the MacKenzies and the MacLeries, a new stability and peace would begin in the western Highlands.

But his gaze always came back to Lilidh.

The love of his life.

The woman who had helped him become the laird he wanted to be.

It always came back to Lilidh and his love for her. One that was threatened by his immaturity and stupidity, but one that was reclaimed in time.

So, at this moment when he should have been the chief and welcoming his important visitors to this significant meeting, the only words he could think of were of and for her. Knowing the pain and the cost of almost losing her, he held his cup in her direction and returned her smile, ignoring all the others there.

'To Lilidh MacLerie,' he began. His throat thickened as he thought of all the things he wanted to say to her, about her, before their kith and kin. All the words vanished until he was left with only those. 'To Lilidh,' he repeated.

The hall filled with cheering and she blushed as they called out her name over and over until it blended together in one roar. Rob reached down and kissed her hand. 'I will tell you the rest later,' he said, pulling her close and touching his mouth to hers.

'Until later, my lord husband,' she whispered back before nodding her thanks to those present.

The meal took some time and hours passed and though Connor and Jocelyn made it their custom to be the last to leave their hall, Rob decided that he would forgo that custom this night. Breaking away from his family and hers, they sought the quiet of their chambers. A momentary stop in the nursery to see that Tavish was sleeping and then he pushed open the door to their rooms.

Before she could walk away, Rob pulled Lilidh into his embrace and kissed her as he wanted to—letting his passion speak to her of his love. As with every kiss, she moulded to him, holding back nothing until they were breathless. He held her face in his hands and gazed at her, thanking the Almighty that she'd given him a second and third chance to come to his senses.

'What did your parents say of the news?' he asked, kissing her forehead and cheeks. 'Were they surprised?'

Her laugh enticed him. 'Mother was thrilled and said she knew. Father...' she paused and laughed again '...Father grunted.'

Rob smiled. He expected no more and no less from his father-by-marriage, though he knew that privately the *Beast of the Highlands* would be pleased. 'And you feel well?'

'Aye,' she said, standing up on her toes to touch her mouth to his. 'This time is completely different from the first.'

He touched her cheeks and lifted her chin as though examining her closely. 'Not a bit of green at all.'

Lilidh stepped back and shook her head as she released the curls from their ties. 'And the strange cravings that I had later in Tavish's carrying have begun already.'

His body reacted, remembering some of the cravings she had that had nothing to do with food as he thought they would have. Nay, she craved...him!

When she tossed her gown and shift to the floor and watched him with hunger in her gaze, he tugged his belt until it dropped, letting his plaid join her garments on the floor. And when his erect flesh was revealed as he lifted his shirt, her gaze heated even more and she slid the tip of her tongue along her lips, sending heat through his blood into every part of him.

He had lost the ability to think at that moment and only discovered it some time later as they lay together in their bed.

'So now the hard work begins,' she said quietly, entwining their hands together.

Rob lost his breath at the thought of more of Lilidh. His flesh answered the call admirably, but her laugh as she pressed her lovely arse against him warned him that he'd misunderstood.

'I meant in the talks. The hard work begins on the morrow now that you have them together.' She turned in his arms to face him. 'Duncan seems to support your efforts. And Rurik as well.'

'Duncan knows the bargain is good for the

At the Highlander's Mercy

MacLeries,' he said. 'Did you hear Rurik call me "Laird"?'

'Aye,' she said. 'Not "Boy" any longer?' Rurik had taken their battle three years ago in his stride, as he always did.

'I have stepped up in his esteem, I think.'

'And once this treaty is worked out, everyone will know how brilliant you are,' she said, kissing him.

That moment in the hall came back to him and he shook his head in reply. 'They should know how brilliant my wife is, since much of this was your doing.'

Lilidh caressed his face and leaned up on her elbow. 'All of this is my doing.'

'All of it?' he asked, attempting to argue when at this moment with her so close he would allow her anything she wished or agree with anything she said, truth or exaggeration no matter.

'I did ask my father to relent and allow you to enter the keep,' she admitted. 'And I did forgive you for your stupidity.'

As she slid her body against his, he nodded. Whatever she wanted...

'And it was my idea that you should seek an

alliance with the MacKenzies.' Whatever she claimed...

She could claim that she had lit the stars afire in the night's sky and he would agree with her, for her leg now rubbed up over his thighs, getting ever closer to... He swallowed against the tightness in his throat as her hand now followed the same path.

'But my best idea was not to follow my parents' custom and wait for everyone to retire this night,' she said, the arousal in her voice making it deeper. He loved that tone.

He rolled then, trapping her beneath him, as he slid between her thighs and entered the place he most wanted to be. A soft sigh escaped her as they joined as one and no other words were spoken for some time. Then, exhausted from the passion they shared, he said the only thing that truly mattered.

'You make me feel worthy, my love.'

Half-asleep, she only smiled at his words. Then, as she fell deeply into sleep's grasp, he pushed the loosened hair from her face and kissed her gently. He knew he would treasure her always for making him worthy of her love.

Always.

* * * * *